TREAT ME LIKE A DOG
(The Band That Time Forgot)

TREAT ME LIKE A DOG
(The Band That Time Forgot)

Dennis Coath

ATHENA PRESS
LONDON

TREAT ME LIKE A DOG
(The Band That Time Forgot)
Copyright © Dennis Coath 2007
'Space Oddity' © written by Davie Bowie, published by Onward
Music Limited.

ISBN 10-digit: 1 84401 869 5
ISBN 13-digit: 978 1 84401 869 7

First Published 2007 by
ATHENA PRESS
Queen's House, 2 Holly Road
Twickenham TW1 4EG
United Kingdom

Printed for Athena Press

Chapter One

Poddy was striding triumphantly towards his van after defusing a wasps' nest. The bold logo on the side of the vehicle proclaimed 'Peabody's Professional Pest Control'. He was now talking animatedly to a client while holding aloft the wasps' nest in a polythene bag.

'Just another job for the exterminator, Mickey.'

'Aye, well, just send us on the bill, Poddy.'

'Yep, job done. We deal with everything Noah couldn't face up to: rats, mice, squirrels, moles, ants, fleas, cockroaches... and wasps!'

'Aye, well, good job we used you and not that useless Noah bloke you were talking about then.'

'Yeah, well, never mind, Mickey. Any road, all those nasty critters have gone.'

'Bloody good job. Sodding well hurts when you get stung by a wasp.'

'Wouldn't know, never been nibbled by one in forty years in this business.'

Lenny 'Poddy' Peabody was to wasps, rats and moles what David Dickinson was to Victorian wardrobes, carriage clocks and silver coffee pots, or Alan Titchmarsh to buddleias, begonias and bougainvilleas. He had built up a thriving business and unrivalled expertise in his chosen profession and passion. If you wanted rid of cockroaches in a kitchen, a mouse in the house or squirrels in an attic, it was a problem Poddy could solve. He claimed to be an 'Oxford professor' of pest control.

'Well,' said Mickey, 'it's nice to see you again, Poddy. You're looking well. Are you still playing in that band, or has age caught up with you like the rest of us?'

'You're never too old to rock'n'roll, Mickey me old son. The Saganauts are playing at the Ferret and Bicycle on Friday night. Then it's Derby v Forest on Saturday. C'mon you Rams! Can't wait.'

'Aye, well, you know where you can stick your Rams and your rock'n'roll.'

'Yeah, cheers. See you, Mickey, and keep it in yer trousers...'

Poddy was still a lad at heart. His life revolved around pest control, rock'n'roll, Derby County football club and his family. Although he had passed sixty-four, he had absolutely no intention of retiring, such was his enthusiasm for his job.

Poddy was in a rush to get home for a special family get-together. He threw the polythene bag in the back of the van and set off. For once he had not been his usual cautious and fastidious self. The bag had not been properly secured and some of the insects were still stirring and waking from a stupor. After a couple of minutes, Poddy was driving along immersed in a cloud of angry wasps. He opened all the windows, but that did not scatter the swarm completely.

After parking the van in the drive of his neat detached house, Poddy sneaked through the back door and ran upstairs to inspect the damage in the bathroom mirror. He now had a bulbous red tip to his nose where a wasp had extracted, or rather injected, revenge. Poddy muttered under his breath.

'Aaaahhhh cowing hell. My bastard snout!'

Poddy still had a shock of curly, greying hair and, despite a bulging girth, was quite fit thanks to the rigours of his job. His wife, Barbara, was still slim and glamorous at sixty, with bold dark eyes, although her raven hair was not quite as natural now. Poddy and Barbara had produced their two children relatively late in life and they were a very close family. Son Buddy was now thirty and back living at home for a short spell, after splitting up with his partner of three years. Buddy made a good living as a musician and local DJ. He also ran a small studio where he dreamed of recording a number one hit. His sister, Bonnie, was twenty-five and worked in London as a model and aspiring actress. Bonnie was married at nineteen and now divorced. She had travelled up from London for a long weekend with mum and dad.

While Poddy was attending to his rapidly reddening and expanding nose, the rest of the family were preparing for a meal and a special treat. Barbara was setting an artistic table, Buddy was clumsily opening bottles of wine, and Bonnie was texting a message to her agent on her tiny mobile phone. All three looked up and stared in surprise as Poddy entered the lounge. At last Barbara broke the silence.

'Bloody 'ellfire, what happened to you, duck? You look like Coco the Clown or Charlie bloody Caroli.'

Bonnie sniggered. 'Jeez dad, I didn't know it was red nose day already.'

Poddy waited for the jibes to die down. 'I had a little problem with a wasps' nest, that's all. I got stung on the snout.'

Buddy replied rapidly, 'God, I never would have guessed, Rudolph.'

Barbara at least offered some sympathy. 'It does look very sore, love. It must be the first time you've ever been bitten.'

'No, first and second time. One of the varmints got me somewhere more painful, stung right through my clothes.'

'Where for Christ's sake?'

'Somewhere you might be pleased about the swelling.'

Bonnie gave a low sigh. 'Oh, dad!'

Poddy then went over to the sideboard and picked up a package that had arrived by special delivery that morning. He handed it to Buddy.

'This is it. It's taken me about twenty years to track this cowing thing down. I eventually traced it to a private collection in New York via a guy who used to work on Pathe News.'

Buddy started to rip open the small parcel. 'So this is it hopefully: the publicity film of the Beatles and the Dogs before the release of your first records.'

'Certainly is. It's the only footage of us and the Beatles after we signed for Parlophone. It was a special publicity shoot. At the time the record chiefs thought we would be bigger than the bastard Beatles.'

'Trouble is,' replied Barbara, 'the bastard Beatles had hundreds of number one hits and your only single reached forty-four in the *New Musical Express*.'

Bonnie was getting impatient. 'Come on, dad, stop pratting about; let's watch the tape.'

The family sat back in awe and amusement to view the forty-five-year-old black and white footage that had been transferred onto a VHS tape. It was the only existing live footage of John, Paul, George and Ringo with Poddy, Streaky, Smudger and Biffo. Exclusive pictures of the four Beatles with the four Dogs.

Poddy got up and pointed to the screen. 'Look, that's me of course, with John. We did a little duet that day on 'Blue Suede Shoes'. And there's Biffo and Ringo with drumsticks in hand. That's amazing: Biffo with long, fair hair. He's as bald as a coot now, the old devil. Streaky doesn't look much different. Paul couldn't believe how good he was on the piano. And there's Smudger with George. I've not seen or heard of Smudger since he upped and left for California. I know he played sessions and got involved in the music business out there.'

Bonnie laughed as Ringo pretended to play a drum roll on Poddy's head. ''Ere, dad, you've got a nose as big as Ringo's now.'

'Wish I had a bank balance as big.'

It was four o'clock in the afternoon, and staff were intently trying to conclude business for the day at the Derby branch of the European Commercial Bank. An ageing hippy figure, wearing a cowboy hat and swathed in denim, sat patiently outside the manager's office. His salt-and-pepper hair was shoulder length, and beneath a neatly cropped beard he seemed to wear a permanent smile. He pushed back the brim of his hat and tried to grab the attention of an assistant.

'"Ground control to Major Tom".'

The assistant looked a bit puzzled.

'Can I help you, Mr Smith?'

'A coffee would be nice, please.'

The hippy figure started playing a few imaginary guitar chords while singing softly to himself, as the assistant produced a coffee from a nearby kitchen area.

'Hey, this tastes cool.'

'Oh, it's not hot enough?'

'No, no, I mean it's real good. Most of the coffee over here tastes like a blend of gravy and motor fuel.'

Mr Smith's accent was a blend of Oxford English and West Coast America. The assistant smiled and then answered a phone.

'Sorry for the slight delay, Mr Smith, but our area manager, Mr Bacon, will see you now.'

Mr Smith looked thoughtful for a moment.

'Yeah, it's all life in the fast lane. Mr Bacon you say, Mr Bacon...'

Something had rung an extremely loud bell in his mind. He walked into the office and gaped at the bank boss, who did likewise. Mr Smith broke into an even broader smile.

'Hey, man, this really is déjà vu! Streaky, my dear chap, the boy wonder on the keyboard, and you haven't changed!'

'Good god – Smudger! I can hardly believe it. What a day! It's been so hectic, what with this and that and now you too.'

'Hey, you look after the affairs of U2? That's cool. I wrote a song for them once. Bono loved it, but they didn't put it on an album.'

'No, no, I meant... No, it doesn't matter. I was so busy I didn't connect Mr Smith with you. James "Smudger" Smith. The last time I saw you was at Watford Gap services. Er, yes: you were having a cup of tea and an Eccles cake.'

'Hey, Streaky, what a memory. For me it's all a bit of a blur. In fact it's fuzzier than that.'

'Which bit in particular?'

'The last thirty-five years or so.'

Streaky smiled. 'So, what have you been up to?'

Smudger eased himself back into the chair. This could take a while. His memory was sharp enough at some things. 'Well, I gigged in LA back in sixty-four. I got together a band – the Coyotes – a bit like the Dogs, only scabbier. Then I formed a three-piece called Moose, and after that a West Coast-style band, the Racoons.'

Streaky butted in: 'Who managed you at the time, David Attenborough?' He laughed at his own, bank manager's joke, but it was lost on Smudger.

'No, I don't recall him. I played sessions with Airplane, Love, the Doors, the Eagles, Linda Ronstadt... and Crosby, Stills, Nash and Young. In fact it was Crosby, Stills, Nash, Young and Smith for a short time. I wrote a few album tracks for Jackson Browne, Willie Nelson, and the Red Hot Chillis. I produced a few albums up in Frisco and managed a couple of bands. Then I went into business with a British-style pub on Long Beach. Hey, I called it the Ferret and Bicycle after that godforsaken pit we used to go to in Derby. Then I did a couple of tours with Springsteen and the Eagles. After that I lived in Laurel Canyon and got involved in the organic food boom. I set up a couple of organic farms with a partner. They are still going OK, but I sold up my share. Now I want to use my contacts to run organic food warehouses over here. You know, take it to the limit, man. You've seen the business plan. It's pretty damn good. In between all that I've been married three times, a few other chicks, no kids to worry about, but I'm single again now. How's the last few decades been for you, Streaky old boy? Remember that final Dogs tour? I wonder what happened to that dancer-chick, Arry, we shagged senseless in Sunderland?'

Streaky looked a little tight-lipped and gestured to a family picture on his desk.

'Arabella is my wife of thirty-eight years.'

Smudger smiled apologetically.

'Beam me up Scotty. No, that's real cool, buddy. No offence, no worries, Streaky. So what have you been up to? You are obviously a successful bank manager and family man.'

'Well, I went back to complete my degree in Economics at the LSE when the Dogs split up and couldn't really decide on anything I really wanted to do after graduating. So I sort of drifted into a career in banking. Arabella and I were inseparable after Sunderland as it happens. We've got two sons – Rupert, who's a chartered accountant, and Harvey, who works as a tax inspector for the Inland Revenue. It's been a big year; I've become Rotary club chairman and captain of Darley Vale Golf Club. Arabella is active as chairwoman of the local Conservative luncheon club. So it's all quite exciting.'

Smudger looked just a little bemused, with a puzzled expression almost wiping out his perma-smile.

'Right, OK... you still play, maestro?'

'Oh yes, I play and practise regularly. It's more Rachmaninov than rock. I do a few classical recitals and play the organ at St Oswald's Free Church. And you?'

'Never gave up. Still the big bad bass man. "Rock and roll, I gave you the best years of my life".'

'Look, Smudger, I don't want to rush you after all these years, but I'm really up to my neck in it. Tell me very briefly about your plans. It all looks sound on paper.'

'Yeah, strictly no risk, man. I wanted to return to Blighty. I've got most of the bread together. It's cool. I want to set up an organic food warehouse. Got the premises in mind. Got most of the backing, the bucks and the business plan. Just need a little bit more.'

Suddenly the phone rang, and Streaky became engaged in a pressing problem.

'Look, Smudger, don't think I'm being rude, but I've got a tricky situation to sort out.'

'No worries, this is a good deal for you I promise. I need to close it.'

'Look, I've got to go, a bit of a crisis with a school governors' meeting. It'll keep me tied up until the early evening, but I can meet you for lunch tomorrow if you like. How about twelve o'clock at the Darley Vale Golf Club. Is that any good?'

'That's cool, old chap.'

'Do you play by the way?'

'No, I don't believe I do, but Alice does… Alice Cooper. And so does Jon Bon Jovi, I think. See you tomorrow.'

Chapter Two

The Ferret and Bicycle had ignored the last few decades so cigarette smoke created a thick fog in the public bar. It was packed with a seething mass wallowing in smoke, sweat and spilt beer. On a low stage along the back wall, Poddy was blowing up a storm on guitar and vocals. The Saganauts finished their final song to a rousing cheer and a long round of applause. Poddy jostled his way through the crowd to join his two drinking and footy mates, Big Eric and Little Jimmy, who had reserved a space and a foaming pint of bitter for him in the corner of the pub. Eric had been employed for years as a bailiff and debt collector. Jimmy was an expert in artificial insemination for farm animals, spending many of his working hours with a rubber-gloved arm up a cow's vagina. The trio had been dubbed the exterminator, terminator and inseminator.

Big Eric pointed to Poddy's nose.

''Ere Poddy, what happened to your bleeding nose?'

'It's not bleeding.'

'It's bleeding red though.'

'I got stung by a sodding wasp.'

Jimmy stopped swilling his beer and joined in.

'Sting?'

'Course it did, stung my cowing nose, stupid.' He quickly changed the subject. 'Any which way, what time are we meeting for the game tomorrow?'

'We're going to get together half an hour earlier. Gonna be a big crowd, probably a sell-out.'

Big Eric ran a huge, fat finger along the back page of the local paper. 'Smethurst's back fit again. You know he broke his leg in three places, Poddy?'

'Where? Blackburn, Barnsley and Burnley?' said Jimmy, laughing at his own joke.

Big Eric piped up again. 'Poddy, Don's coming along with us to the match.'

'Oh god, no – not Don "spend a night in the cells with me" Conway?'

'The very same.'

'Yeah, I remember that Leicester game. Don tried to walk off with one of the corner flags under his arm. Any which way, this copper says "What have you got under your arm?" Quick as a flash Don says, "Hairs; what have you got, feathers?"'

In James 'Smudger' Smith's mind he was still a student in the sixties. In reality, he was now sixty-one, but had never really grown up and never really intended to. He always referred to blokes as 'cats' and girls as 'chicks'. In many ways Smudger lived in a time warp. His years living in wacky California hadn't helped. After nearly forty years with only the odd fleeting visit, he was a little out of touch with the British way of life.

Smudger was dressed in a brown fedora hat, big buckled boots, denim jeans and a fringed denim shirt as he walked into the reception of the Darley Vale Golf Club. The receptionist looked up in some surprise as Smudger started to speak.

'Can you hear me Major Tom.'

'You want a Major Tom?'

'No, Captain Streaky. I mean Captain Bacon.'

At that moment Streaky walked through the reception area, immaculately attired in the golf club blazer and tie, white shirt and grey flannel trousers. He looked at Smudger as if he were a down-and-out at a Buckingham Palace tea party. 'Look, Smudger, you can't come into the Captain's Lounge dressed like that.'

Smudger looked himself up and down rather quizzically, before Streaky fumbled out an embarrassed explanation.

'No… You see… Well, I should have told you. You have to wear a tie. Ever since the Captain's Lounge opened in 1929, no man has entered without wearing a tie. Even the plasterers who came to fix one of the cornices had to wear ties.'

Smudger was amused. 'I don't think I've owned a tie since class 5A at school.'

Streaky rummaged in a box under reception and found a brand new golf club tie, still in a cellophane sheath. He presented it to Smudger, who tied it theatrically around the collar of his fringed denim shirt.

'I'm sorry about this, Smudger. It may seem odd to you, but it is a famous tradition here.'

Smudger grinned and burst into song. '"A white sports coat".'

Smudger followed Streaky down a corridor, through to a plush lounge that looked like a location aboard an old ocean-going liner. The walls were covered with golf pictures and portraits of famous players. There was also a huge plaque listing the past captains. The roll of honour started in 1889 with Algernon Roseberry-Hide and ended in 2003 with Brian Bacon.

Streaky was still a little put out by Smudger's appearance. 'I've ordered some tea and coffee and sandwiches. That OK with you?'

'That's cool. Look, I'm sorry about the gear. The chick on reception looked at me as though I'd asked to murder her granny.'

'No, no, that's all fine now. And Smudger, I've checked through your business plan. I didn't realise how many assets you have. You've done rather well for yourself.'

'Yeah, won some and lost some.'

Streaky nodded in approval and tapped the file in front of him thoughtfully. 'Now look. I've got some ideas, but I don't want you to think I'm going to tell you how it's going to be. It's—'

'"You're gonna give your love to me",' said Smudger, as quick as a flash.

Streaky relaxed and broke into a smile. 'The plan is very sound. I've checked everything through and there are absolutely no problems with the security you've got. I see you still own a property in Los Angeles.'

'Oh that; it's a little place out in Laurel Canyon with a minia-ture studio. I let it out recently to Joe Walsh, Coldplay and the Dixie Chicks, and quite a number of other bands as well. It's a great place for cats to chill out and write and rehearse.'

'Well, I must admit you've got me and Arabella "onside".' Streaky made inverted comma signs with his fingers, to show how hip he was. 'We both eat lots of organic produce. All the local supermarkets stock it. Can't get enough.'

'I'm going to take things a bit further down the line. I've got exclusive rights to all sorts of exotic substances.'

'Yes, I remember you smoked most of them.' Another bank manager's joke. Smudger grinned.

'No, I mean melons, star-fruit, papaya, pineapples, pomegranates, passion fruit. You name it, I can get it from farms in California. In the end I made more money from melons than music.'

'Never saw you as a businessman, but it all looks pretty impressive.'

'Well, you have to be sharp in LA, especially in the music business. Everyone tries to rip you off. By the way, do you keep in touch with the others, Poddy and Biffo?'

'Yes, they're still around. Biffo retired about five years ago.'

'He still whining and complaining about every goddamn thing?'

'Well, I don't think he's changed. He went on to complete a teacher training qualification and taught history at the General Gordon Comprehensive for about thirty-five years. Always said he hated it. Actually, he still hammers away on the skins in a local jazz and blues band. I've seen them; they're very good. But Biffo still looks bloody miserable behind the drum kit.'

'And what about dear old Poddy?'

'I look after his accounts. He set up his own pest control business back in the sixties and has made a few bob, or a few bucks. He's something of an expert in the field. Doing really well.'

'Really, and does he still play as well?'

'What, Poddy! He's the life and soul of the party, still. He could compete with you for the title of Britain's oldest teenager. Poddy plays these rock'n'roll nights in a couple of pubs. His son Buddy does a bit in the music business, has his own studio. I look after his accounts, too.'

Smudger stroked his chin with his left hand and seemed preoccupied for a moment. The smile had given way to a thoughtful expression.

'So all the cats are still jamming, gigging and grooving, huh? So let's all get together for a bit of fun. Come on, Streaky. "It's only rock'n'roll but I just love it".'

'No, I don't think so… As I said, I'm more Bach than, er, Blur these days.'

'So I'll take that as a "yes". Good to do business with you, old chap.'

Poddy was on his rounds, talking to a couple about a rat trapped under their kitchen floorboards. The discovery had left them so shocked they would probably have been happier if it was a live grenade.

The woman was particularly upset. 'Of all god's creatures, rats are the most disgusting, unlovely things.'

Poddy begged to differ. '*Ratus ratus*,' he began.

The woman looked even more disgusted. 'You mean there's two of them?'

'No, *ratus ratus*. That's the Latin name for the brown rat. They're not as evil as people make out. Rats are very devoted mums, or rather the female ones are.'

The woman was getting more frantic and flustered. 'Try mothering that and you wouldn't have any fingers left. What are you going to do, for heaven's sake?'

Poddy produced a spray can from his bag with 'Rodent Deodorant' written on it.

'No worries any which way. The rat's dead and its corpse is under your floorboards. Now if we leave it, it's going to stink the cowing place out. To save you a lot of cost and all the bother of ripping up the floorboards, I spray this through a small hole. Then the rat decomposes quickly without the slightest odour.'

The couple looked doubtful. Poddy ceremonially brandished the can.

'By the way, don't spray this under your armpits. It's Peabody's Patent Rodent Deodorant, my own magic formula.'

'Is that it? Is that all you're going to do? Make it smell nice?'

'Trust me, I'm the Exterminator. It'll work. I'll do the job in two shakes of a dog's tail and send you a very small bill.'

At that moment Paddy's mobile phone rang loudly with its rock riff ringtone. Poddy walked out of the house and listened to the voice at the other end, paused and then exclaimed, 'Smudger! Well, bugger me backwards with a bog brush.'

Buddy Peabody was sitting cosily in the front room with a fresh pot of coffee, reading an electronics magazine, when his father burst in looking flustered and excited.

'Buddy, my boy, what's the chance of me and a few of the lads borrowing your studio tomorrow night for a little session?'

'You and some lads! Who?'

'Me, Streaky, Smudger and Biffo.'

'Jesus, it's sodding pensioner power.'

'You're cowing right it is!'

Streaky was sitting in his expensively draped and upholstered lounge, eating olives and drinking a fine Sancerre. Arabella looked up from behind the local paper.

'I see that Squiffy has finally split from Suki. Never knew what she saw in that oily little runt in the first place. Gosh, Dot and Maurice are celebrating their golden next month. We should be invited. You know that ghastly little man Fornswater, he's up on a gross indecency charge next week. By the way, Cynth and Nigel have asked if we can make up a four for bridge at their place tomorrow night.'

Streaky countered abruptly, 'No, no. Very short notice. Can't make it. Doing a musical night.'

'Is that a rehearsal for the Beethoven concert at the town hall?'

'Well, no, not really.'

'Oh… well, what is it?'

'Just a little practice.'

'Who with?'

'Oh, just some old friends.'

'What old friends? You haven't got many old friends, or young ones for that matter.'

'Oh, just a group of musicians.'

Arabella was getting angry, the more evasive Streaky became.

'Well, *who* for god's sake? Spit it out.'

'Well… There's Lenny Peabody, James Smith and Charlie Bear.'

Arabella gave a searing glare that could have welded steel. 'Are you joking? You must be.'

'Look… It's just that… Well, Smudger has returned and we just—'

'I thought the Dogs had been exterminated, destroyed, put down, gassed to death and shot about forty years ago. What the hell are you doing with those deadbeats again at the age of sixty?

The mangy, pox-ridden, dog-eared, shitty Dogs.'

'Look, Arry, there's no harm in it. It's just for one night at a little studio, that's all. Just a get-together for a bit of fun.'

'And don't tell me, a few beers with the lads? So that's why you can't play bridge with Cynth and Nigel. The flea-bitten Dogs.'

'Look, darling, it's just a bit of fun. Just a bit of fun, that's all.'

Arabella gulped a glass of wine and looked agitated and angry while Streaky sheepishly chewed the last olive. There was an uncomfortable silence.

Chapter Three

Buddy Peabody had a compact studio in a cellar below a shoe factory. It was called the Sole Studio. Buddy was meticulous in looking after his equipment and preparing for a recording session. Bonnie Peabody, who was also fascinated by the Dogs' reunion, was sitting alongside Buddy at the control panel. Buddy flicked open a couple of faders.

'Well, we're all set. Just got to wait for Dad and the old codgers to arrive.'

'Is this going to be embarrassing, bro?'

'Well, no, they're all still good musicians. Well, you've seen dad play guitar and sing. Brian Bacon does classical concerts as well as my bank accounts.'

'What about the old guy on drums?'

'Oh god, Charlie Bear: Biffo. He came in this afternoon to set up his kit. He's about as happy as a hung-over sow with chronic haemorrhoids. He's sixty-five, acts about eighty-five and looks about a hundred and five. He's like Charlie Watts' great-grandfather.'

'Who's the other bloke?'

'That's James Smith. He's the main reason for this soirée. Pissed off to America after the Dogs broke up, so dad says. That was forty years ago. Now he's decided to come back. Probably got the FBI on his tail. He's like something out of *Easy Rider*. Watch out, he still really fancies himself.'

'He'll get a stiletto in the bollocks from me if he tries anything.'

'He's an extraordinary character. Played with lots of top bands, or so he claims. Now he's set up some sort of big export deal with Streaky.'

'What's he exporting, cocaine and marijuana or Sanatogen?'

The door to the studio opened and an old man in a shabby anorak shuffled in. Buddy greeted him cheerily.

'Biffo, old chap. The old man told me you'd be first to arrive.'

Biffo stubbed out a needle-thin roll-your-own. He had a bald, domed head with long, grey hair at the sides and back, and a pair of black, horn-rimmed glasses.

'Thought I'd get here early in case anyone pisses around with my drum kit. Did a gig at this pub up near Manchester, had a fookin' half-hour break, came back and some fookin' kid was pratting around on my kit. Fookin' bastard. I hope this is going to be productive and not some useless piss-about. I don't like wasting my time.'

Bonnie went into a small galley kitchen to make some coffee. Buddy tried to brighten up Biffo's mood but pressed the wrong button.

'Still, it's going to be great, isn't it, to see Smudger again after all these years.'

'Smudger... Smudger Smith... Smudger fookin' Smith... Smudger fookin' bastard Smith. That randy sod, he'd shag a chocolate frog if he could stop it melting. Me and Smudger never got on. I haven't come to see that git. Just hope this is going to be worthwhile.'

Poddy, who had heard most of Biffo's comments, walked in with a guitar under his arm.

'Fancy catching you complaining, Biffo, and we haven't even started the cowing session yet.'

'Well, I'm only here because of you, Poddy.'

Buddy was fascinated to meet Biffo for the first time.

'Tell you what, Biffo, you're about as cheerful as a prize bull with its bollocks caught up in barbed wire.'

'No, young man, I just don't enjoy playing unless it's musically worthwhile. I mean I play regularly with very good musicians, and I know you do, Poddy, but I don't know if Smudger and Streaky are up to scratch. For all I know they can't play a fookin' note.'

'They're better than ever; just enjoy yourself, Biffo. Have a laugh now and get it over with. Remember, Streaky could have been a classical scholar. It'll be great having a reunion any which way.'

'If I want a reunion I can have one with my old teaching colleagues or jazz band or local labour club.'

'Great thing about you, Biffo, is you'll never change. Once a whingeing old git, always a whingeing old git.'

Next into the studio was Smudger, brimming over with enthusiasm and joie de vivre. He walked up to Biffo and gave him a big bear hug. Biffo was taken aback by the bonhomie.

'Blimey, last time I remember you was with that dancer in Sunderland. You were virtually shut off in your fookin' room with her for days.'

At that moment Streaky walked in, looking very uneasy and unsure of himself. Smudger interrupted quickly. 'Don't remember that, Biffo.' He pointed at Streaky with two fingers. 'Hey, don't shoot me, I'm only the piano player.'

Streaky smiled weakly. Poddy was working at double time, trying to break the ice. He produced a pack of cold beers, cracked some open and offered them around. Streaky treated his can like an incendiary device. Meanwhile Smudger lit up a huge joint and took a deep suck. Streaky looked horrified.

Smudger strummed an acoustic guitar and kept repeating '"Light my fire!"'

Poddy was anxious to try to lighten the atmosphere. Biffo and Streaky were as tense as virgins in Ibiza and stiff as starched corpses.

'Come on, gang. The Dogs are back in Derby for one night only. Let's just warm up with a corny twelve-bar like "Can I Get a Witness".'

Biffo pretended to give a deep yawn. 'Oh fookin' great, really fookin' great. I've come all the way for that.'

Smudger stubbed out his joint and smiled wider. 'Look, Biffo, old boy, I've come all the way from Los Angeles, not Loughborough for this gig. Come on, boys, let's get it on.'

Buddy tried to organise the band, with a little help from Poddy. They left Biffo to his own devices to set up his drum kit. Streaky started to relax, and even enthused about the piano tone on the keyboard. He warmed up with a bit of Scott Joplin and then let rip with a Jerry Lee Lewis impression. This had the effect of kick-starting the Dogs into action. The first numbers were surprisingly good as they ripped through a few old standard rock'n'roll numbers. Biffo's jazz-style drumming and Smudger's nimble-fingered bass underpinned the band. Streaky's fingers were a blur on keyboards, and Poddy led from the front with rasping vocals and strident guitar. The Dogs were putting on a show.

Buddy called for a break. Poddy and Smudger slapped palms in a high-five celebration. Even Biffo seemed to be smiling, although Poddy wasn't too sure.

'That a smile, Biffo, or is it wind? Come on, lads, that was fantastic. Cowing hell.'

Bonnie walked into the little studio, applauding.

Smudger whispered rather too loudly into Poddy's ear, 'Hey Poddy, who's the foxy chick?'

'That's my daughter, Smudger. Stick to Saga slags.'

Smudger looked reproachful, and the smile slackened a little. The band listened to their rendition of 'Summertime Blues' that Buddy had recorded, and slugged from the cans of beer. For something jammed, without a rehearsal, it was a clever treatment. Poddy snapped his fingers.

'Hey, remember that song we must have rehearsed about a million cowing times, that was going to be a single—'

Smudger burst in, singing:

> Cos you treat me like a dog
> Treat me like a dog
> You got me yelping and yapping, snarling and a snapping
> Cos you treat me like a dog

Streaky started to hum. 'My god, I remember it well. I composed that and Poddy wrote the words. It was good.'

Biffo also recalled the song. 'Good? That was fookin' crap.'

'Don't sit on the fence,' said Poddy. 'Tell it like it is.'

The band started to play a few bars of 'Treat Me like a Dog', then paused. Buddy made a few changes to the arrangement. Streaky then added a stylish piano part. They played through the song several times. After several re-workings, Buddy was happy. Even Biffo was not grimacing too much. After the drum roll on a final chorus Buddy exclaimed, 'That's a take!'

The session ended hysterically with lots of broad smiles and backslapping. Smudger exclaimed, 'Just a few licks from the Dogs! We're back; we didn't ever break up. Just had a forty-year vacation.'

Chapter Four

The Dogs wound up their first recording session since 1963 and sat round in a circle in Buddy Peabody's compact studio. Poddy dished out cans of Marston's Pedigree. Smudger tore open a ring pull and filtered the beer through his drooping moustache.

'Hey guys, it's a heck of a long time since I had a drop of 'Peddy'. This is the nectar of the gods, man. One thing you can't get in California, along with curry and chips, and sex standing up in a bus shelter late at night.'

Smudger slurped from his can, put it down, grabbed an acoustic guitar and started strumming and singing. Poddy swiftly provided the next line to the song. Soon the Dogs were singing in harmony. Streaky was relaxed and necking his third can of beer. Even Biffo appeared to be happy. Poddy slapped him on the back. 'C'mon, Biffo, you wouldn't have missed this for the world.' Biffo felt a little caught off guard and abruptly checked his spontaneous sense of enjoyment.

'Well, it was better than I ever imagined it fookin' could be. I've been playing regularly with top-class musicians so I wasn't too sure about you blokes. Still, rock'n'roll's kids' play anyway, compared to jazz. Any bastard can play this sort of stuff.'

'Yeah, and you've just proved it, Biffo old boy,' countered Poddy. 'And Streaky, we've got you out of the house and given you a break from Beethoven and Bach. Nice to see you released from captivity. I'm surprised Arabella doesn't have you tagged. Sightings of you and Biffo are about as rare as Elvis singing with Pavarotti in the Ferret and Bicycle.'

Smudger was misty eyed and in a reflective mood. 'You know, this is the best scene. It's always cool, these little impromptu sessions. Just get a few cats together. Nothing much planned, just jamming. I remember one I did with Jim Morrison, just with acoustic guitars, formed the basis for some of the Doors' first songs. Did this session with Hendrix once in an old cellar in sixty-six, with me on bass and this one-legged Mexican guy on drums. And I remember this mega jam with Janis Joplin on a tour in this old fish-canning factory.'

Biffo yawned. 'Aye, and they've all prospered since. Is there anyone still alive you played with? You weren't Buddy Holly, Glen Miller and Otis Redding's fookin' pilot as well? Any road, I've got to get back. Sylvia will be waiting up, and I've got to take the Labradors for a walk.'

Biffo left without so much as a goodbye. The others stayed on chatting, drinking beer and strumming guitars before leaving the studio.

It was past midnight and just Buddy and Bonnie remained.

'Shall we go back, bro?'

'No, I just want to do a few things with that recording. I'm going to add a rhythm track and beef up the bass sound.'

Buddy worked for three hours mixing and re-mixing 'Treat Me like a Dog'. It was while he was trying to find the best version that he heard Biffo moaning between takes. Biffo was a genius at whingeing and could almost make it sound like poetry. Buddy stopped the tape. That was it, he thought to himself. Biffo's moaning monologue was like rap – well, pensioner's rap – all done in that whining Midlands singsong voice.

> *Treat me like a dog – it's a pile of shite*
> *Don't matter 'ow much we play it, it won't be right*
> *Can't call it music, it's not like jazz*
> *Let's give it a rest cos I need a wazz*

It was bizarre. The words had nothing to do with the song; in fact it was one long stream of negative comment about it. But it worked. Buddy lifted Biffo's words and laid them between verse two and the chorus. Then he moved Streaky's piano break. He worked for hours. Eventually he'd finished, and he was pretty pleased with the final result. Bonnie had nodded off on the sofa while he worked. He nudged her awake.

'You know what, just for a bit of fun I'm going to send this to Duke Deckster as a possibility for his record of the week.'

'Don't be daft, more like dinosaur of the week.'

'Only for a laugh. He'll remember me. Before he became famous we compèred together as DJs at a three-day festival. This could be Duke's Diamond.'

'More likely to be Duke's old duffers.'

'Come on, Bonnie, it's not that bad. In fact, I think it's very good.'

The next morning Buddy was enjoying a cup of coffee with Poddy, eager to play him the final recording. He clicked the CD into the player.

'Now, dad, listen to a modern masterpiece.'

He hit 'play' on the CD player, and father and son sat back in silence for three minutes. When the song ended there was complete hush. 'Well,' said Buddy.

'Well what?'

'What do you think?'

'What, are you telling me that's us? I thought you'd put the wrong track on!' He smiled at Buddy's look of disappointment. 'It's all right, son, not bad at all. But you'll have to do it again – I can hear Biffo moaning in the middle of it.'

'But that's supposed…' Buddy realised he wouldn't be able to explain, so he changed tack.

'I'll tell you something, dad: Streaky is an extraordinary piano player.'

'He bloody well should be. When he was about fifteen he was one of the top piano scholars in the country. That's a belting sound. Jesus, are you sure that's us?'

'Well, I've put in quite a bit of production and sort of fattened the sound.'

'Makes my croaky old tonsils sound a bit better.'

'It's a mix of the modern idiom with Old World charm and my old man.'

'No, it's just a corny old bit of rock'n'roll, son – I'd can it if I were you.'

Chapter Five

Sunday evenings had developed into a tradition for Duke Deckster. After a late afternoon lunch, he listened to a batch of new releases accompanied by his partner, Juliette, and a couple of bottles of vintage champagne. Over the past five years 'The Duke' had built up his breakfast radio show on UKFM to a daily audience of nine million – by far the biggest rating for any radio show in the country. The Duke had used a string of publicity stunts to power up his profile. He had created plenty of column inches in the tabloids and appeared on a vast number of TV shows. The result was that he enjoyed a cult status across the country. His morning show was a brilliant act of quick-fire wit, comment and charm that appealed across the generations. The Duke had dubbed himself 'the hit-maker from Kingston, Jamaica'. In truth the nearest he had been to Kingston, Jamaica was Kingston on Thames.

The Duke was born in London in 1970, the son of the Jamaican ambassador. His real name was Gilbert Winstanley. Gilbert had grown up in leafy London suburbs like Pinner and Northwood and went to Eton. He was a gifted scholar, and a top-class university career beckoned, but Gilbert had started dabbling in extracurricular activities during the long school holidays. Much to his parents' annoyance he started work as a late-night jock at the age of nineteen and never looked back.

On air he spoke in a mix of Cockney and Jamaican patter. In real life his accent was cut glass English. The contrast between the private man and his public alter ego could not have been greater. Extrovert, ebullient and theatrical over the airwaves, Gilbert was refined, reserved and cultured to his close friends. Duke Deckster was all lager, laddishness and largeing it. Gilbert Winstanley was more interested in claret, cuisine and the classics.

His weekly mission, as he relaxed in his Little Venice apartment, was to choose 'Duke's Diamond' from a stack of CDs.

Juliette, who headed up her own PR company, helped with his selection. As usual the Duke had been badgered and besieged by reps and pluggers who wanted their product to be chosen as his record of the week. It ensured ten plays on the UKFM breakfast show, and that sort of airtime guaranteed a top ten hit and more often than not a number one. In the music industry, Duke's Diamond was the holy grail.

The first batch of discs only lasted a few bars each before the Duke pressed the eject button.

'I say, Jules, my little honeydew melon, can we chill this fizz just a tad more?'

'Sorry, Bertie darling. I was in a bit of a rush. I'll just pop it in the freezer for five minutes. Don't think much to the stuff you've played so far. It's all dreadfully dull and dreary.'

The Duke played a few more songs that got the thumbs-down, then pulled a letter out of a package.

'This could be interesting. It's from Buddy Peabody – haven't heard from him for years. We worked together at this festival in some goddamn awful spot in the Midlands a few years ago. Not a decent restaurant for miles. Really capital chap though, Buddy. He went into recording and DJ-ing and all that sort of stuff. Now he suggests I ought to listen to his new band.'

Juliette picked up the CD and grimaced. '"Treat Me like a Dog" by… the Dogs. Hmm, doesn't exactly sound too promising.'

'That's what they said to Wagner, Jules, about *The Ring Cycle*.'

The Duke played the Dogs disc all the way through, and even showed a little interest.

'That's actually pretty refreshing, but maybe not quite the ticket. I'm not sure Duke Deckster would fancy that, although Gilbert Winstanley does. It's weird; it reminds me of some of the sixties' British rock bands we used to listen to in the dorm at Eton, like the Yardbirds, the Animals and the Stones of course. Really odd, like the sixties brought up to date – really love that weird rapping in the middle, really innovative.'

The Duke waded through a few more songs and sipped champagne. 'Poor stuff this week, Jules. That agent, Miles, has been trying to foist this band on me called Complete Head Cases. I'd marginally prefer to listen to two pigs having a farting contest.'

'Oh Bertie, that's gross. I've put another bottle of Pol Roger in the fridge. Come on, it's nine o'clock and you haven't come up with a winner yet.'

'Tell you what, Jules old thing; I'm going to give a hearing to that Dogs track again.'

The Duke sank back into a voluminous leather armchair, closed his eyes and listened intently.

'Clever bit of piano, gravelly vocals, good dance beat and the rap thing. Umm, it's quite catching.'

The Duke repeated the CD for a third and then fourth time of asking, and then sprang to his feet to replenish his champagne flute.

'That's the one. That's it. It's very, very catchy and the sound is so unusual.'

The Duke was now humming the chorus.

'It's sort of sixties with modern recording techniques and an almost classical piano sound. It's like Manfred Mann, or the Moody Blues meet Eminem. That's definitely the one, Jules. Let's crack another bottle of Bolly.'

Poddy was holding court in the corner of the Ferret and Bicycle with Big Eric and Little Jimmy. The exterminator, terminator and inseminator were in session over a line of empty pint glasses. The trio were planning for a cup match away to third division Blodworth. Poddy was less than enthusiastic.

'Last time we went there we were frisked for weapons before going into the pub near the ground. They wanted to check we had some. It was a right dump. There was a sodding pig in the corner of the club bar as an air freshener.'

Big Eric guffawed and wasn't about to be outdone by Poddy. 'They say Blodworth has been twinned with Grozny and Grimsby in a suicide pact.'

Poddy came back quickly. 'Yeah, in Blodworth they have guys riding shotgun on the bleeding milk floats.'

Jimmy was looking lovingly into his ale. 'The way we're play-ing we couldn't beat Barnsley pork butchers' third team, let alone Blodworth.'

Poddy groaned. 'The last time Derby won a cowing cup trophy, Dick Turpin robbed the coach on the way home. 'Ere lads, did you hear the story about that new striker Atkins? They say he was delighted to be offered a cortisone injection. Thick bastard thought it was a high-performance car.'

The trio chortled in the corner. Poddy was in full flow. 'The way we've been playing over the last few seasons, Lord Lucan could have been hiding in our midfield. Any which way, who's for a pint?'

Poddy already knew the answer; he was halfway to the bar as he posed the question. As he returned with three foaming pints and sat down, Jimmy looked at him inquiringly.

'Hey, I know what I forgot. You never told us about your get-together on Friday night and the return of Smudger "Shagger" Smith. How did it go?'

'No bullshit, I'll tell you it was brilliant. Biffo was a pain in the arse, so nothing new there, but I think the old git really enjoyed it, although he'll never admit it.'

Big Eric put down his pint. 'So what about James Smith? Last thing I remember about him was him giving that French assistant one behind the bike sheds, before he was expelled for popping amphetamines during assembly.'

'Well, it livened up the hymns. Never sung "Onward Christian Soldiers" so rapidly. Any which way, Smudger still looks the same... only older. He's mellowed, and I suppose he's returned to this cowing place to set up a business. But I reckon he's on the run from a string of ex-wives and girlfriends in America. He's a year younger than me and acts like he's Britain's oldest teenager. Must have made a shed load of cash over the years. He's renting a luxury flat and a big fuck-off 4x4 jobbie.'

Jimmy interrupted. 'What about Streaky?'

'He was as happy as a dog with two dicks by the finish. Mind, so would you be if you escaped from the dreadful Arabella for a night. He did this fantastic Jerry Lee Lewis impression. You know what, he can play absolutely anything and everything. We even recorded this old song which I wrote with Streaky forty cowing years ago.'

Big Eric tremored with mirth.

'I expect Duke Deckster will play it as his Diamond on UKFM tomorrow.'

'Yeah, ha sodding ha, Eric. Anyway, I've got an early start tomorrow. What are you two deadbeats doing?'

Jimmy laughed. 'I've got to service a load of Friesians up near Belper.'

Big Eric added, 'And I've got to escort some flea-bitten squatters off some premises in the city centre.'

Poddy drained his pint glass. 'I have a mission with *Mus Musculor* at 8 a.m. That's the house mouse. Got to go to a big Victorian terrace that's overrun with the things.'

Big Eric looked interested. 'We've had them bloody things, so what's the best way to get rid of them?'

'Best method is to employ or adopt a big psychopathic moggy and let the bastard loose. Otherwise it's Poddy's patent TTs, or Tiny Traps. I work out where their runs are and strategically place a series of them around the house, baited with ripe strong cheddar. The whole key is the positioning, and that only comes with years of know-how. You see, they're crafty little sods. Got to get inside their minds. Then wallop!'

Over the years Poddy had grown to respect many of the pests he had to eradicate. He saw his task as control rather than extermination.

'Clever little chaps, house mice. They're very adaptable. Feed on just about anything we leave behind and make nests in every little nook, crack or cranny. So, I'm exterminating mice, you're terminating squatters and you're inseminating Friesians. Nice work if you can get it.'

Chapter Six

Poddy was always awake at half past six and brought Barbara up a cup of tea. He faced a half-hour journey to Burton upon Trent that morning. The Pestmobile, as he called his van, was equipped with all sorts of traps, cages, ropes, ladders, nets, poles, sprays and poisons.

Poddy normally approached a pest control problem with the intensity of a chess master planning his strategy, but in the car in the morning he was a constant channel hopper, listening to a variety of radio stations. He enjoyed digesting the news on Radio Four and Five, and catching up with local news on Radio Derby. Since being introduced to Duke Deckster's breakfast show by Buddy, he frequently listened to UKFM for the slick presentation of banter, comment and music. Poddy had just heard a financial report on Five Live and switched to UKFM for a little light relief.

The Duke was working up a head of steam ridiculing one of the lighter stories dominating the tabloids that day. Poddy chortled at his take on the tale of a young starlet who had emerged from the sea in Corfu not realising that water made her bikini completely see-through. Deckster followed with some quips about a vicar caught with his trousers down at a parish party. Poddy was grinning to himself and enjoying the show. Then the Duke announced, 'It's five to eight and this is really great. You've been waiting for this: it's Duke's Diamond. It's the band that time forgot. I can tell you this will just cruise up the charts. It's bound for number one. "Treat Me like a Dog". This is the Dogs!'

Poddy nearly swerved off the road. He slowed and steered into a lay-by, listening on his car radio to the song he had written with Streaky four decades ago. It was never really meant to sound like this. Sweat was now pouring down his face. The Duke finished the CD and played a reverberating jingle saluting his 'Diamond', with a reminder that you could hear it again at five to nine.

Poddy was stunned. He sat in the car for fully ten minutes just staring at a nearby cornfield before dialling Buddy.

'Did you hear that?'

'Certainly did, dad.'

'How the cowing hell did it happen?'

'I sent off the recording to my old mate Duke Deckster, and the rest, as they say, is history.'

'More like sodding fantasy.'

'Nine million people probably heard it.'

'And he plays it all week twice a day?'

'That's the deal, dad.'

'Well shag me sideways.'

'No thanks, dad.'

'I mean, I'm just bloody gobsmacked.'

'Well, we've got to work quickly.'

'Christ, what's next?'

'This guy from Jet Records has been on.'

'At this time in the morning?'

'Yep. Woke me up at seven thirty. Duke Deckster tipped him off. You see, people already – yes already – want to buy "Treat Me like a Dog", and there's no record deal. But they can do an express job and have the single in the shops for Wednesday morning.'

'Jesus, son, this is all a bit overwhelming, and I've got a load of mice to sort out.'

'You can spare the mice for a while. What about this record deal? I've negotiated a few and this sounds good.'

'Well, we'll have to have a meeting and see what the others think.'

'Of course they'll agree to the deal; there could be a lot of money in this. Look, we haven't got much time to discuss it for Christ's sake. I'm the producer, you're the co-writer. Let's just give it the OK. Tell the others when it's all done and dusted. Trust me, dad. Trust me!'

'If you say so. I feel dizzy. I need a cowing lie down and I've got to go and set a load of mousetraps.'

Poddy rang off and slumped in the driving seat of the van. He chewed a peppermint. He was feeling delirious and disorientated. Was this really happening?

It certainly was, and happening rapidly. At ten thirty Buddy had taken command and met a representative from Jet Records at Watford Gap services on the M1. He handed over the original recording and signed a deal. The record was scheduled for rushed release on Wednesday morning.

Thanks to the patronage of Duke Deckster, an extraordinary domino effect accelerated sales of the Dogs' disc. UKFM staged an on-air game of 'pass the parcel' as the Duke gave the CD to morning presenter Ron Jon and he in turn kept the chain going. By midnight 'Treat Me like a Dog' had been played seven times on UKFM.

On Tuesday morning Jet Records rushed out samples to radio stations. In his column in top-selling magazine *The Comet*, Duke Deckster tipped 'Treat Me like a Dog' to be a surprise chart-topper. By this time, folk as varied as workers on building sites, students on campus and brokers at the Stock Exchange were singing the catchy canine chorus.

> *You treat me like a dog, treat me like a dog*
> *You've got me snarling and snapping, yelling and a yapping*
> *Cos you treat me like a dog*

By the end of the week the song had registered a British record for the number of airplays. On that Wednesday morning the scene in London's Oxford Street was replicated all over the country. The music stores had 'Dogs CD on sale' signs in their windows. Queues began forming before the shops opened. People from every generation bought copies.

Chapter Seven

'Now for the tricky bit.'

It was Wednesday evening, and Buddy was talking to Poddy outside his Sole Studio. Buddy had hastily convened a meeting with his father, Smudger, Streaky and Biffo. He had phoned both Smudger and Streaky and explained the situation. At first they both thought it was a practical joke; when the penny dropped they were both astounded. But Biffo was completely oblivious to the events of the past few days. Poddy pushed Buddy towards the small double doors into the studio.

'Let's try and keep the mood very calm, son.'

'Whatever the guys think, they could be in line for a bit of a windfall, or at the very least a few quid.'

As they walked in, an aggravated Biffo was first to speak.

'What's this all about? One fookin' session was bearable, another will be like having my fookin' toenails pulled out with rusty pliers. I was forced on pain of death to come here.'

Buddy held up his hands. 'No, no, no. I've not got you all together for a session. Smudger and Streaky have got a fair idea of what's been going on, but I just haven't been able to get hold of you.'

Biffo was getting more and more indignant.

'This seems to be building up to the sort of mess where I need to call my fookin' solicitor.'

Smudger waded in to try to pacify Biffo. 'Look, old chap, just stay loose and chill out. We're about to hear some good news. We could have a little extra bread coming our way.'

Poddy burst in, 'Look, everyone, just hush and let Buddy explain.'

Buddy embarked on a long and rambling explanation about the extraordinary number of airplays that had led to the rush release of the Dogs' CD, and how he had had to sign a swiftly organised, but potentially lucrative, deal with Jet Records based on sales. Buddy was keen to stress that he had acted in everyone's best interests and thrashed out very good terms.

Biffo still could not comprehend what was happening.

'You're trying to tell me that silly song we recorded only five days ago could be in the fookin' top ten? Bollocks, this is too daft for words.'

Streaky remained stiff and silent. Smudger again intervened. 'Look, old chap, we're all trying to take this in. Strange as it seems, it was made record of the week on UKFM and then it all sort of exploded.'

'Well, how should I fookin' know? I only ever listen to Radio Three and Jazz FM.'

Buddy made another attempt to calm Biffo down.

'Look, I've negotiated with record companies before. I'm telling you, this is a mega deal, but it depends on sales. That's the only gamble and it's an odds-on shot, if I've read the form correctly.'

On Thursday morning Duke Deckster, on his breakfast show, was the first to announce, 'This is incredible; you are witnessing history being made. After one day's sales, Dukes Diamond is glittering at number one. You heard it here on UKFM first. It's yappy, wappy and snappy and I'm the chappie who let the Dogs off the leash.'

At the offices of *The Comet*, editor Dick Rodger turned off the radio and summoned his showbiz correspondent, Fiona Clamp. Rodger was wizened, skinny and neurotic; Fiona was a hard, vamp-like blonde with a tiny waistline that accentuated her 34F bust. Rodger was known as Rick Dodger, or 'dick-brain'. Fiona was known in the press as 'Twin Peaks'. Rodger had a nervous habit of swilling coffee from a polystyrene cup and speaking at the same time. He was very agitated that morning. There were drips of coffee on his chin.

'Right Fiona, this is one of the biggest music stories since the Beatles. We've got to nail this one down. This band has had a record number of airplays and now has the fastest-selling single of all time. It was even featured in a story on Radio Four, for Christ's sake. Who are they, what are they, where the fuck are they?'

'Nobody knows who the fuck they are or where the fuck they are.'

'Well, you'd better find out. I want them on the front page tomorrow… exclusive!'

'So far I've run into a load of shtum people. They all seem to have taken vows of silence. It'd be easier to find the incredible shrinking man with a bus load of aliens on Brighton beach.'

More coffee dribbled from the sides of Dick Rodger's mouth. 'We did that last week. It's odd, you know; their sound seems like something dated, yet up to date.'

'I've still got a few calls to put in to some contacts in the music business, but it all seems to be top secret at Jet Records. I just can't explain it. But I'll sort the bastards out.'

Fiona Clamp displayed the resolve of a starved Rottweiller eager to get its teeth into a big, juicy bone. She stormed out, leaving Dick Rodger chewing his polystyrene cup and flicking through *Horny Babes*, one of the Comet Group's glossy magazines.

Events had been unfolding quickly; now everything and everyone was on fast-forward. There was no chance of pressing the stop button now. Jet Records had decided at an executive meeting that the Dogs would be unveiled to an expectant public on Friday night's 'UKTVTOP10' show, which was to be hosted by Duke Deckster. As part of the arrangement the old boy band were to be kept in a secret location. Security was to be tight. The band would record the song on Friday lunchtime, lie low until after the show, and then be presented at a huge press and media bash.

So the Dogs, still in a state of shock and disbelief, were to remain incognito from Thursday afternoon until Friday evening, under the custody of Jet's public relations and media officer Olivia Ponsonby-Smart. Olivia, tall and stick-like, with auburn hair and rimless glasses, had strict instructions to keep the band hidden away in a small country hotel in the Chilterns. As part of the deal, they would be cut off from communication. Strictly no mobiles, although Biffo had never owned one and despised their use anyway.

Olivia took on the job as mother hen to the fading four. Poddy, Smudger, Streaky and Biffo were not really sure whether they were in the dock waiting to be sentenced, or about to find Shangri-La in the small hotel near Leighton Buzzard that had been commandeered for their exclusive use.

Luckily for Olivia, Biffo was strangely subdued and, by his own standards, quite content. He was sat in a corner with a pot of tea and a plate of chocolate biscuits, studying a book on the Battle of Trafalgar. He had the blessing of his wife, Sylvia, and had figured that any stress and strain would be worth it if he could finance the conservatory he had always wanted. Olivia strutted around, trying to keep her charges happy. Poddy needed no cheering: he was enjoying the adventure immensely. Streaky, however, was tense. He'd had a horrid task explaining the course of events to Arabella. As for the bank, he had told them he had to sort out urgent family matters in London for two days.

Olivia was arranging the Dogs' dinner. 'I've instructed the chef to provide a range of starters. We've got seared tuna, vegetable lasagne and roast beef for main courses. I thought that would cover all tastes. Then there's a sweet trolley, fruit and cheese. Now, would anyone like a drink?'

Poddy thrust his hand upward like a schoolboy at the back of the class.

'Please miss, that's an easy one. A pint of bitter for me and Biffo, and a gin and tonic with ice and lemon for Streaky, I believe. And what about you, Smudger?'

Smudger's smile sprung open a little wider.

'I thought you'd never offer. What about a really fine claret, if it's all on Jet Records? Why don't we share a bottle, Olivia?'

When the drinks arrived, Biffo continued reading in a corner, engrossed in Nelson's naval tactics. Poddy and Streaky started a game of chess, while Smudger sprawled at ease across a settee, waiting for Olivia to reappear. She returned and sat upright in a chair. A waiter followed her and went into the adjoining room with a tray of drinks.

Smudger looked appreciatively at Olivia and then in turn at the bottle of wine and two glasses on the tray.

'Very impressive, Olivia. Château Margaux.'

'Glad you approve. By the way, everyone calls me Oops.'

'Oops? Why, is your second name Daisy?'

'Daisy?'

'Yeah, like oops-a-daisy.'

'No, nothing like that. It's very simple, I've had the nickname from my first day at school. You see, my full name's Olivia Olga Ponsonby-Smart. Olga was my Russian granny. So I've always been Oops.'

'So how long have you been with Jet, Oops?'

'Oh, it seems a lifetime. I just can't get out.'

'You can check out, but can't leave, huh?'

'Let me see… I joined as a junior rep after leaving college at twenty-one and I've been with the company now for eighteen years. Part of the furniture.'

'Yeah, but you're more like a deluxe velvet armchair than a threadbare sofa.'

'What about you? Someone told me you once met Elvis.'

'Met him! I taught El to play harmonica, back in sixty-nine. I had a little jam at Graceland with some cats. Me, El, Lenny and Chas.'

'Lenny and Chas?'

'Yeah, John Lennon and Charlie – Charlie Watts. We finished with a barbie in the garden at Graceland, roasted the biggest hog on a pile of logs.'

Oops' expression was a mix of mirth and admiration. Behind her, Biffo yawned and got up from his seat.

'Never heard such a load of bollocks. Nearest he's been to fookin' Graceland is probably cloud cuckoo land. Anyway, I'm up to hit the hay early.'

Biffo traipsed out, leaving the others in the lounge. Poddy and Streaky were engrossed in their game of chess, while Smudger continued to beguile Oops with his stories from the sixties and seventies. After an hour, Poddy and Streaky decided to retire early as well, leaving Smudger, Oops and another bottle of Château Margaux.

Oops was genuinely fascinated by the Dogs phenomenon.

'I've put together a file of your CVs for the press conference on Friday night. I never knew that the Dogs were launched by Parlophone on the same day as the Beatles. You were stable mates.'

'Yep, it was meant to be us, could have been us and should have been us. Back in the days when I was younger, well I'm still a puppy dog now. We were better musicians I reckon, but they were better songwriters and prettier. Well, even the elephant man and the hunchback of Notre Dame were prettier than Biffo, let's face it. But that was then and this is now.'

'Didn't you feel a bit jealous?'

'Naw, they were great cats, but I've had my moments in the music business.'

'But you've made your fortune from melons and mangoes.'

'Yeah, from my session work and royalties I saved a few bucks and went into a consortium with some other musicians, marketing and distributing stuff from organic farms in California. And the business hit the big time. That's why I came back to Blighty, to set up a similar scene over here and escape the chasing pack.'

'Oh? And what, or who, are they?'

'Well, nothing too serious... Tell me, Oops, why isn't a chick like you permanently shacked up with some guy?'

'Well, I was for some time, but we split and I've been so busy for a few years that I've only had a few casual relationships...'

'They're the best kind.'

'Oh, so you're a love-a-chick-and-leave-them sort of cat, eh Smudger?'

'Sure, "I'm a strummer, I'm a drummer, I'm a rover and I'm a groover". No way, sometimes I dream of sitting round the fireplace every night with the same chick, a big dog and a glass of red.'

'Well, you're not getting any younger.'

'Well, I think I am! These days I do lots of workouts and meditation. It used to be freak-outs and medication. Anyway, I'm in great shape for sixty.'

'Sixty-one, according to your CV.'

'Well, I subtracted one. Don't be pedantic, Oops, and pour another glass of that red. Good for the health, the heart and the blood.'

Oops drummed her fingers on an unusually large watch face.

'Remember, big day tomorrow. It's all got to be tickety-boo.'

Smudger snapped his fingers in the direction of a barman at the other end of the lounge.

'Well then, let's celebrate our success. Hey, fella, can we have a bottle of bubbly and two glasses?'

Smudger turned back towards Oops. 'I suppose this is still all on your mob?'

Oops nodded. 'I suppose so.'

'Well then, let's make it vintage stuff.'

The barman reappeared hastily with the bottle and two champagne flutes. Smudger grabbed the tray.

'How about one in my room?'

'I'll have one in your room. One glass of champagne, that is, and that's all. Then, James Smith, it's time for all good boys to go to the Land of Nod.'

'What about the bad boys?'

'They join the good boys.'

Smudger and Oops walked stealthily up the main staircase and slipped quietly into his room. He carefully detonated the champagne cork in his right hand and filled two flutes.

'Cheers, Oops. Here's to the Dogs and Jet Records.'

They chanted in unison, 'The Dogs!'

Smudger's big smile expanded all the more.

'After all, we are top of the charts.'

'And with a big fat royalty cheque to come. Sales have shot up even more today.'

'You know, even at my age it's all a bit bewildering.'

'Well, you've adjusted well. Poddy seems OK. Takes it all in his stride. Streaky is sort of excited but a bit suppressed and so tense. As for Biffo, he seems permanently pissed off, and he's about to make a shed load of cash.'

'Tell me about it. Me and Biffo have never exactly been like Starsky and Hutch, or Yogi and Boo Boo.'

'So what makes him tick, for Christ's sake?'

'Wind, bile, bitching, complaining and whining. But he's comparatively placid at the moment. He's actually realised there's money in this whole shebang.'

Oops replenished the flutes, removed her glasses and slipped off the clip to let her lush auburn hair cascade over her shoulders. Smudger took a deep breath.

'Jeez, Oops... Wow, that's a magic split-second makeover.

"Devil in disguise or my special angel, babe".'

'So am I more of a chick like this, Smudger?'

'As we used to say many years ago in class, that girl's something else.'

Oops finished her glass of champagne and put it down.

'Look, I'd better go back to my room now. I shouldn't really be here; you're one of my clients, although you are a nice stray dog.'

'Woof, woof, baby.'

Oops sniggered and decided to refill the flutes. Smudger embraced her loosely.

'Let's go to bed, Oops.'

'We'll go to bed. But I want to sleep. There's no rumpy-pumpy or hanky-panky.'

Smudger gestured to a luxuriously linened king-size bed.

'No problem. Plenty of territory for both of us.'

'Actually, I hate to sleep alone, but you keep your pants on, you dirty dog.'

'Don't worry. I'll keep the boys in the barracks and the missiles in the silo and get some zeds in.'

Oops tiptoed somewhat unsteadily across the room, and draped her black Jil Sander suit over an armchair, stripped down to her matching silk thong and bra, and slithered under the sheets with Smudger. Within seconds they had lost consciousness.

Chapter Eight

Friday had been planned with military precision by Oops. The timetable was tight. She awoke with a start and a throbbing head and saw it was five to nine. She shoved a slumbering Smudger in the back and yelled in his ear, 'C'mon, we've got to move quickly. It's rendezvous in the breakfast room at nine.'

Smudger was a little incoherent. 'Hey babe, this is getting like a boot camp – 9 a.m. is like the crack of dawn to me.'

Smudger and Oops frantically threw on the clothes they had shed the previous night and rushed out of the door at the same time that Biffo and Streaky were vacating their rooms down the corridor. Biffo looked angry and pained, Streaky rather puzzled. Oops was first to the punch.

'Come on, chaps, I've had to burst into Smudger's room to wake him up. At least you are wide-awake. He looks comatose.'

Oops went into mother hen mode.

'Now everything will go smoothly today if we keep to time. I have built a little leeway into the programme. We've got an hour for breakfast. Then the coach picks us up at ten thirty. We rehearse at the UKTVTOP10 studios at twelve and record the song for transmission at one. Then we come straight back here for a break, then back up to London for the press conference after the show at eight.'

The Dogs sat down for breakfast with their minder. Everyone was apprehensive, but Biffo was squirming around in his chair looking particularly disturbed. He was sitting by the window with Smudger. Streaky and Poddy were discussing stage positions with Oops. Smudger gulped a cup of coffee and looked at Biffo's strained, red face.

'You don't look too well, old man. What's the matter?'

'If you must know, it's me fookin' Chalfonts.'

'Chalfonts?'

'Me fookin' Farmer Giles.'

'Farmer Giles?'

'Do I have to fookin' spell it out for you? Haemorrhoids.'

'No, I don't believe I could spell that.'

'Piles, fookin' piles.'

'Yeah, I get it now. Pain in the arse huh?'

'It's fookin' agony. I couldn't sit on my drum stool. Like red-hot grapes.'

Biffo summoned Poddy over and whispered in his ear. Poddy then relayed the problem to Oops.

'Look, we need a doc, and quick. He really is in agony. Says he couldn't play in his current condition. He looks absolutely buggered, poor old git.'

Oops dialled her office to get them mobilised. They returned the call to say that a doctor with knowledge of the urgency of the occasion, and treatment of the condition, was on his way from Leighton Buzzard and would be at the hotel before ten.

Biffo went up to his room. Poddy ushered Dr Stone, a stern-looking young man, into the room. After a thorough examination he addressed Poddy and the stricken Biffo.

'Now look, I'm going to give you some cream to reduce the swelling and I want you to apply an ice pack. Then, because your manager has informed me of the importance of the day, I'm going to give you an injection of morphine to kill the pain. We'll need to monitor the situation when you return this afternoon.'

Biffo was in some distress, but by the time they boarded the people carrier with blackened windows the effects of the injection had started to kick in. As they reached London, Biffo was starting to feel delirious and look manic, but the agony had decreased to mere pain. The Dogs sailed through the rehearsal. They could play the song on automatic pilot but, in fact, they didn't have to; all they had to do was mime. By the time of the recording for the show, Biffo's grey hair was virtually sticking out at the side, accentuating his bald dome. He was clenching his teeth and had a wild, faraway look in his eyes. It didn't stop him moaning though, and fortunately his mumbling seemed to fit the rap section of the song perfectly.

In the studio gallery director Rikky Hazard was calling the shots.

'Camera two, stay on the drummer, get in a little tighter. Fucking hell, he looks like a mad Methuselah. How old is he, ninety-five? Go to one. Two, give me an even closer shot of the geriatric drummer. Go to three. Back to two. He's out of his skull. Look at his eyes.'

The song finished with a rapid drum roll. Rikky Hazard turned towards his producer in the gallery.

'That really was out of this world. We've had the fab four; this is the fucking fearsome foursome. It's amazing, but they can really play and the drummer looks like he should be in a home for crazed centenarian drug addicts.'

Oops was watching from the corner of the gallery and made a discreet phone call to Dr Stone.

'Hello, yes, it's Olivia Ponsonby-Smart. We'll be back early, just after two. Biffo will need another morphine injection I should think. OK, see you later.'

Unfortunately, a nearby technician, Billy Budgen, had overheard the call. As Olivia left the studio he sidled up to Rikky Hazard. 'A word in your ear, Rikky. The mad old guy on drums is on morphine.'

'Well, he was certainly on something. How do you know?'

'I just overheard that skinny publicity bird telling someone. Gospel, mate.'

'God, he was on another fucking planet. Couldn't half play though.'

'Yeah, he wants another fix this afternoon.'

'Thanks for the info, Billy.'

By the time the Dogs returned to their country hotel hideaway, Biffo was squirming in pain again. Dr Stone was waiting in the lounge and ushered the uncomfortable drummer to his room. Biffo returned after an hour's treatment. The doctor decided he would need another jab before they set off for the press conference at half past six.

The old boy band tried to relax by watching television, drinking tea and eating chocolate biscuits, but they were startled by a trailer that was appearing before every ad break.

'It's exclusive on UKTVTOP10 tonight. It's the fastest-selling song in British pop history. It's a debut for the Dogs, the mystery band, and you'll find out their bark is as good as their bite tonight at seven thirty on UKTV.'

Poddy, Smudger, Streaky, Biffo and Oops watched in awe as they realised the nation's fascination in their unmasking before millions of TV viewers that night.

Back at the UKTVTOP10 studios the press were gathering for the show. Jet Records were sponsoring a big media binge, and the Dogs were to be unleashed on the press at eight o'clock. Fiona Clamp was furtively moving amongst the various groups, carrying her champagne, when she noticed Rikky Hazard subtly trying to catch her eye.

'Hi, Rikky, how's it hanging? There's a rumour going around that these guys are really old gits.'

'They are, but I've got something even better. Usual deal?'

'Well, depends what it is.'

'It's a bloody cracker. The old drummer, who looks about a hundred and twenty-five, is on morphine. He was zapped for the recording and looks out of his head. You can't fail to notice. It's amazing.

'You're absolutely sure?'

'Certain of it.'

'Usual deal. That's fantastic. The drugged geriatric drummer. The drugged old Dog on the drums.'

The bash to unleash the Dogs was strictly organised and tightly controlled. Jet Records were keen to retain the band's mystique. There were to be no individual interviews, although large sums of money had been offered. Scribblers and snappers were told there would be a short photo shoot, followed by a press conference. The band was to sit on a raised platform and field questions from a voracious gathering of journalists and reporters. There were even newspaper writers and TV crews from America and several European countries. The Dogs' tale had spread across two continents. Every media representative was presented with an information pack and a free CD of 'Treat Me like a Dog'.

The press were gathered in a large studio, watching the recording of the UKTVTOP10 show on big plasma screens, presented by Duke Deckster. At the start of the show, few were watching the images, preferring to scoff canapés and wash them down with champagne. A gaggle of freeloading journalists could make vultures around a carcass look quite sophisticated in their etiquette. But now the tension was starting to build. The unknown mystery band that had soared to the top of the charts with a catchy song that everyone was singing and humming was about to be revealed. The show was set for record audience figures. Everyone wanted to see the faces behind the band that had shot to number one, thanks to an unexpected publicity campaign and the mushroom effect of record airplays. Newspapers had been ferreting around for the past three days to lift the veil of mystery, but Jet Records' campaign to conceal their identities had increased expectations. In truth, fewer than twenty people knew who the quartet were, and they had been sworn to secrecy.

It was five minutes to eight. There was an explosion of fireworks and special effects. Duke Deckster heralded the nation's new number one and suddenly the Dogs burst onto the screens.

One reporter choked on a prawn canapé. Two spat their out champagne. The Dogs rocked into action like four old boys at a bus queue leaning against an electric fence. The press corps was stunned, speechless... spellbound. It was a superb performance.

Treat me like a dog
Like a good old dog I'm trusty and true
Baby I'm just far too good for you
You give a whistle and I come running
I'm just faithful and you're so cunning
Cos you treat me like a dog
Treat me like a dog
You've got me yelping and yapping, snarling and a snapping
Cos you treat me like a dog
I go for walkies when you tell porkies
Cos when the fur flies you tell lies
Your bite's much worse than your bark
You've got me groping in the dark
Cos you treat me like a dog
Treat me like a dog
You've got me yelping and yapping, snarling and a snapping

Cos you treat me like a dog
I'm just a poodle, you're like a hound
I'm on the leash when you're around
C'mon baby just stop that nagging
All you need is to get my tail wagging
Cos you treat me like a dog
Treat me like a dog
You've got me yelping and yapping, snarling and a snapping
Cos you treat me like a dog

Poddy led from the front, moving like a man with itching powder in his overalls. He looked jolly with his curly grey hair below his ears and jowls wobbling as he powered out the vocals. He strummed the chords frantically on a black Fender Stratocaster balanced on his burgeoning beer gut.

Streaky was neat and nimble on the keyboards. He looked even taller, skinnier and more gaunt with his distinguished steel-grey hair slicked straight back.

Smudger was hardly moving a muscle, throbbing his bass guitar and grinning like a Cheshire cat with a bowl of cream and a fresh salmon. His white-flecked hair dangled to his shoulders under a Fedora hat. Before the recording he had clipped his beard to stubble, but his moustache was still big and bushy.

But it was Biffo who was the centre of attention, mesmeric and manic on drums. The pain he was suffering made him look more haggard, his bald pate gleaming, blue eyes bulging and cadaverous features a strange, putty-coloured hue.

The scenes of disbelief at the press conference were being replicated up and down the country. In living rooms, pubs, clubs, hotels and college common rooms people were gasping and gazing in amazement at the unveiling of the most antique band in pop history.

As soon as the UKTVTOP10 press screening was finished, Duke Deckster triumphantly ushered his protégées into the reception, where he was to compère the press conference. The four musicians sat down to a spontaneous round of applause from the gathering. They sat behind a long table on the stage, Poddy gleaming, Smudger grinning, Streaky grimacing and Biffo glowering.

Fiona Clamp was whispering to *Comet* photographer Darren Spivey. 'Dazza, just get me a couple of wide shots, then loads of close-ups of the drummer.'

'Which of the old gits is the bastard drummer?'

'The oldest git, Charlie Bear.'

'He looks more like old grumpy bear or bald grizzly bear.'

'Just get lots of close-ups of him now, forget the others.'

'OK, Fi!' Darren Spivey clicked and flashed frantically with two cameras.

The press conference got underway with Smudger tapping a mic and saying 'Can you hear me Major Tom?' Business began with Poddy and Smudger answering a stream of questions. Oops had really embellished and embroidered the CVs of the band in the press handouts, and the journalists were searching incisively for an angle. They probed Poddy with questions about pest control.

'How do you catch a rat?'

'Get a sadistic Jack Russell or give me a ring, pal.'

They were keen to find out who Smudger had collaborated with as a session musician in California. Smudger smiled, exhaled loudly, thought for a few seconds and began, 'Well, there was El, Elt, Lenny, the Boss, Jacko, Eric, Mick, Keith, Jimi, Kurt, Stipey, Bobby, Shezza, Carlos, the Dead, Big O, Stevie, Bono, Youngey, the Mac, the Knack and the Shack. Plus a few others I can't recall.'

The band were interrogated at length about their beginning with the Beatles. Streaky and Biffo remained silent and uneasy. At last it was Streaky's turn to answer a question as the mood lightened and a journalist piped up from the back row, 'Mr Bacon, can you give me some financial advice?'

Before Streaky could answer, Poddy butted in, 'Yeah, never take advice from a bank manager who plays in a rock band.'

Streaky at last burst into a smile and politely replied to a few questions. Lastly the attention turned to Biffo, the retired history teacher and jazz drummer. His answers were tense and abrupt.

'Charlie, you taught history?'

'Yes.'

'What sort of history?'

'General history.'

'Didn't you specialise in anything?'

'Yeah, teaching history.'

'What have you been doing since you left teaching?'

'Nothing. I retired.'

Biffo was not proving very forthcoming, but Fiona Clamp was chuntering away in Darren Spivey's ear. 'Dazza, get some shots while he's talking.'

'Talking, is that what you call it?'

'Just get as many close-ups as you can.'

'Cheerful, talkative old tosser, isn't he?'

'Life and soul.'

'Through this lens I can see the blackheads on his nose and a wart on his forehead. Play your cards right, Fi, and you could pull.'

'Piss off, Dazza. At least he'd be a better shag than you.'

'Yeah, once he's ripped off his incontinence pants.'

'Anyway, Dick Rodger is going to love this stuff. You're shooting a big, big scoop.'

'Well, I am aware of that; this lot are just about the biggest freak to hit the top of the charts in history.'

'No, we've got something else, Dazza. Our little old drummer boy you're taking pics of is drugged up to his eyeballs. We've got that little line exclusive.'

'Fucking 'ell, no wonder he looks like a demented alien. Blimey, his eyeballs are nearly out of their sockets. Well, I was going to say he looks like a mad dog.'

'You said it. Good line, Dazza.'

Oops had instructed Duke Deckster to wind up the briefing after half an hour, which he did, much to the chagrin of the hack pack and media mob. As the Dogs turned tail, the Duke ended the conference by proclaiming, 'I told you this would be a massive hit. It's even bigger than the Duke dreamed. Now that's a fact. Tonight you've seen the band that time forgot.'

Chapter Nine

The Dogs were guided back to the blackened-out people carrier to be transported to their Chilterns hideout. Poddy and Smudger were quite ecstatic about their new-found fame. Streaky was bemused and Biffo confused.

At the hotel, Oops called them together for a meeting with Jet Records' chief, Godfrey Vanderbloom. Streaky and Biffo, who had taken a lot of persuading to perform the number one hit and attend a press conference, were now getting quite agitated. They were to be reassured by Oops and Godfrey.

Godfrey Vanderbloom exuded authority. He was a veteran of the music business. 'God', as he was known by everyone, was in his late fifties and had started as a tea boy in Tin Pan Alley. He was fit, thin and distinguished-looking, with neatly cut fair hair streaked with grey. God was dressed from head to foot in sharply tailored designer clothes. He addressed the band in a small reception room in the hotel. Oops towered by his side, teetering on thin stilt-like heels. The news that the exploits of the band had already made a considerable amount of money made Streaky and Biffo feel more enthusiastic about the Dogs' surprise reunion.

God rarely wasted words. 'Now, your manager Buddy, I believe he's your son, Lenny?'

'Yep, that's my boy.'

'He's signed a short-term contract and a very good one, purely on the basis of this one release. He's a smart operator your lad, Lenny. Now, thanks to Duke Deckster and the explosive effect of a load of DJs championing the song, it's gone to number one. You've also had the record number of airplays in a week by a long way and a record number of sales. You've got a fat cheque to share in royalties already. We're going to send you a little down payment, shall we call it?'

There was silence while the facts sank in. Biffo grumpily bawled out, 'Well, why didn't someone tell us all this before?

Then we'd know all this fookin' poncing around was worthwhile.'

God held up his hand reverentially.

'Well, Charlie, everything was very sudden and totally unexpected. So far, events have happened too quickly to keep up with and control them. We're now catching up. I bet you guys can't believe what's gone on.'

Smudger laughed. '"Planet earth is blue, and there's nothing we can do".'

God continued. 'Now, what I propose is a contract for three more singles, an album and a tour. But no doubt you'd want me to sort that out with Buddy, if he's your manager.'

All four nodded in agreement.

The dozing Dogs enjoyed a lie-in before coming down to a late breakfast on Saturday morning. Even the broadsheets had featured the unmasking of the Dogs on their front pages. The tabloids had spread the story over several sheets.

Most of the coverage was complimentary. There was the odd jibe about them being a 'crock'n'roll' band, but 'pensioner power' was the most popular line and a cliché that was certain to stick. The band's musical ability had been praised. There was even a Dogs poster on page three of one tabloid, pushing a topless glamour model down to page five.

Over teapots and toast racks the band turned to *The Comet*. Its front page featured a close-up of a staring, wild-eyed Biffo. The headline read, 'DRUGGED OLD DOG ON DRUMS'.

Biffo threw the paper down in a fury. 'Fookin' 'ellfire!'

Chapter Ten

Jet Records' publicity machine, principally Olivia Olga Ponsonby-Smart, moved into overtime and overdrive. *The Comet*'s exclusive about Biffo was countered by the story about how the brave old drummer boy had to take powerful painkillers to combat an agonising back (and not backside) ailment. The headlines turned to praise of the courageous sixty-five-year old, who had played through the pain barrier to entertain fans. Suddenly Biffo was acclaimed as an ageing rock hero. All the intense publicity had one simple effect: the Dogs' record sales shot up even more.

The band faced three days of hectic recording sessions. They polished up a version of 'Can I Get a Witness', rehearsed a few prospective album tracks and cut a follow-up single they wrote and recorded in just three hours, called 'Doggone'. The quartet were then given three days off to go home, relax and try to come to terms with the events of the past couple of weeks, before starting a busy schedule involving recording an album and going on a nationwide tour. Buddy Peabody, Godfrey Vanderbloom and Oops held several meetings and decided the policy was to strike while the iron was still white hot and make it molten. The tabloid interest was fanatical.

Poddy had always been a stable kind of bloke, but even he found it hard to come to terms with the events of the past few weeks. He returned home to a champagne celebration with his proud family, followed by a reunion with his mates in the Ferret and Bicycle.

He entered the public bar under a huge banner – 'LENNY PEABODY: PEST CONTROLLER AND GERIATRIC ROCK STAR'. Big Eric was first to greet him, with a slap on the back that nearly shattered his spine.

'Told you it would be record of the week.'

Poddy burst into laughter. 'Cowing right you did, but if I

remember correctly you were taking the piss at the time.'

'Bloody right I was.'

'I'll tell you one thing, it was a bigger surprise for me than you. Biggest bleeding surprise I've ever had.'

Little Jimmy shook Poddy's hand vigorously.

'Well done, mate. Saw you on the TOP10 show and you made Mick Jagger look young.'

'Well, he is, compared to Poddy!' said Eric.

The exterminator, terminator and inseminator had been re-united with something to celebrate. Big Eric already had the party in full swing.

'There's a pint of Peddy winging its way over to you, Poddy, as we speak. Hey, a Peddy for Poddy. 'Ere, what's the low-down behind that business about Biffo being a fucking junkie?'

'Don't believe that crap, Eric. Poor old sod had cowing piles. He was in some pain I can tell you. The doc had to come along and give him an injection.'

'What, up his arse?'

'No. In his arm. The pain was in his arse.'

'Well, he's always been a pain in the arse.'

'He's always been a complete arse. Poor old bastard. That's all that happened. Then, for publicity purposes, the record company said he had a pain in the back and not backside. Any which way, what's been going on round here?'

Jimmy pondered for a while.

'Do you remember that Vic that used to come in here?'

'What about him?'

'He's been crashing out in the rest room at the glue factory.'

'Why, is he addicted to sniffing the cowing stuff?'

'No, he's got nowhere else to go. He was giving that poodle-clipping woman, Mavis, one on the side – has been for a while if truth were told – but his missus got wind of it.'

'Not Mavis with the funny twitch?'

'Yeah. He was at Mavis's flat above the poodle parlour until very late one night and staggered home absolutely rat faced. Now, when he got in, his missus was only bloody well waiting up. So Vic pretended to act as though nothing had happened. Then, when he took his coat off in the hall, he had no trousers on.'

'Bit of a giveaway, eh?'

'Just a bit.'

'So, what happened?'

'She booted him out there and then. He went back to Mavis's and she told him to sod off an' all. So he went back to the factory and got one of the security guys to let him sleep in the storeroom.'

'Well, at least he's sticking to the job.'

Big Eric guffawed with laughter. Poddy signalled to the bar, and three more pints were being pulled.

Poddy turned to Big Eric. 'So, I've missed the last two games and by the look of it I've not missed much.'

'No, that young lad from Wimbledon in midfield couldn't trap a dead rat. The striker from Sweden, Stig what's-his-face, couldn't head a large balloon. The only one doing any good is Buncey, and he's always on the bench; he'll get fucking piles like Biffo. They've nicknamed him "the Condom". They slip him on, he does the business and is then withdrawn.'

Streaky had spent an uneasy night with Arabella, who was not sure how to react to her husband's sudden fame. In the morning they sat around the kitchen table with tea, toast and the morning papers. Arry frowned and scowled as she turned over a page in the *Financial Times*.

'Oh my god, there's even a full page article on the scabby Dogs in here, with pictures of that hideous Biffo and that smirking hyena Smudger. Can you believe it? I mean, what is happening? I've got a Conservative ladies' coffee morning tomorrow. Brigadier Aubrey-Awston's wife is coming along. I'm almost too embarrassed to go.'

Streaky sighed and looked slightly helpless, as if looking for a prompt.

'Well, I can't help it. This all just happened. Well, it just has. Look, I'm steamrollered by it all, darling. I haven't had time to draw breath.'

'I wish that Smudger never had. Has he had a couple of face-lifts to give him that horrid smile?'

'No, he just doesn't seem to react to all that's happened at times.'

'That's probably all the strange substances in his system. He must be like a walking laboratory.'

'No, no, he's a pretty fit chap these days.'

Arabella sniffed and sipped her tea.

'I mean, just how can I explain to Mrs Frobisher-Nelson that the piano player in the mangy Dogs is my husband?'

Streaky ignored the comment and read out aloud from the article in the newspaper.

'Hmmm, this is good. "Keyboard player Brian Bacon gives the Dogs their unique sound with a light classical touch to embellish the band's solid rock sound." That is good, excellent.'

Arry snapped at the corner of her toast and at Streaky.

'When are you going back to work? This silly business has gone on long enough. I mean, what is the bank going to say? And what have you got out of all this so far, apart from meeting up with a load of deadbeats again?'

'Well, I've taken three weeks' vacation that I'm owed.'

'I didn't want you to go to that so-called get-together with Biffo, Poddy and that sickly, slimy, smiling Smudger in the first place, ugh! You know this could seriously affect your standing in the bank. You know that Smithson mentioned you could be in line for an executive national position. Then there's your standing in the local community. I mean, even young children are singing and chanting that banal song.'

'Well, I wouldn't say it was that bad, Arry. After all, I did write the music for it about forty years ago.'

'Well, let's hope this frightful escapade is over quickly and we can get back to some semblance of a normal life. Anyway, I'll go and get the mail; I'm expecting a catalogue from Harrods.'

Streaky was cheered by another enthusiastic review of the Dogs in another paper, while Arry returned with a pile of letters.

'Anything interesting in the mail, darling?'

'Well, there's an electricity bill. That's gone up again. And let me see… Oh, I thought it was my mag from Harrods, but it's your golf magazine. There's a note from Hilda about a flower arrangement class, and there's a letter from Jet Records with a payment. At least you've got something out of the Dogs' dross. It's a payment for… payment for… payment for…'

'Payment for what?'

'It's a payment for two hundred and seventy-five thousand!'

Streaky pretended to be calm and blasé.

'Yes, that's just the down payment we've been waiting for.'

'Why didn't you tell me before?'

'Didn't want to worry you.'

'Well, that's fantastic! We can clear the little bit outstanding on the mortgage and get that apartment in Puerto Pollensa.'

'I thought it was Dogs' dross?'

'No, no, maybe I was a little harsh. Golly, it's not that bad, darling. Actually, the church warden's wife thinks it's rather good.'

'By the way, I'm taking early retirement now and leaving the bank.

'Yes, well, come to think of it, I suppose you are. I mean, why not?'

Charlie Bear had just returned from an early morning walk with his two Labradors, Perkin and Lambert. The pain in his backside had now subsided to a mere ache. He was pleased to find no reporters or photographers outside his house after being besieged for two days. Biffo had refused to do any interviews or pose for a photo with Perkin and Lambert, and had badgered the local police to clear away the press pack on the pavement. While Biffo enjoyed complaining, his wife, Sylvia, was a cheerful, conciliatory soul.

'C'mon, love, I'll wipe Perkin and Lambert's paws; you sit down and I'll get you a nice big pot of tea and a bacon buttie. It's your favourite smoked back bacon from the butcher's. Are your piles playing you up, luvvy?'

'No, Sylv, that ointment seems to be doing the trick, really shrunk the bastard things. Have you seen my biography of Rasputin?'

'It's on the top of the telly, love. You must have had a good walk; Perkin looks exhausted.'

'No, it was a bloody lousy walk. I had to talk to that stupid woman with the glass eye that lives down the road in Wickley Woods. Then some snappy little thing that looked like a fookin' dirty white mop tried to bite Lambert's leg. So I kicked it in the bollocks. Should have kicked the owner. Oh, and have you seen that anti-social, brain-dead idiot next door has started some crap extension? Then some bloody reporter tried to collar me in the park. I told him to fook off. Bloody nerve.'

'Never mind, luvvy, here's your Rasputin book and you've got a letter. It's from Jet Records.'

Biffo grumpily fumbled with the envelope and finally ripped it open. He pulled out a cheque and examined it for a few seconds.

'Fookin' 'ellfire!'

Chapter Eleven

Smudger had become the subject of a major number of press inquiries, his alleged sessions with Elvis being the main drawing card. Jet Records' policy had been to restrict publicity to keep up the 'mystique', and let little morsels slip out slowly to be snapped up by the predatory reporters.

Fiona Clamp bustled into Dick Rodger's office, her protruding breasts acting as a kind of aerodynamic foil as she cut through the air. Dick Rodger put down that month's edition of *Horny Babes* magazine and guzzled from a chewed polystyrene cup.

'Dick, we need an exclusive with James Smith.'

'He's Poddy in the Dogs, isn't he?'

'No, Smudger.'

'They all sound like they stepped out of *The Beano*. What's the score?'

Fiona flipped open a small note pad.

'I've just spent a bit of time making enquiries with some journos in California. He was a bit of a legend by all accounts. Now, in the Jet Records CV it alludes to the fact that Smudger has been married once. He's been fucking married five times and had a shed load of other affairs and partners. He makes Mick Jagger look like a tranquillised tomcat with one testicle.'

'Sounds like a week's series of stuff. Got any chat from any of his former women?'

'Want a few samples? Let me give you a few quotes. "Smudger had a mighty manhood; we made love all night in a sleeping bag at the top of the Grand Canyon." That was Kasha, a ballet dancer he was married to for a year. Oh, and how about this one? "Smudger liked making love in public places. We did it under a towel on Malibu beach, in a crematorium garden of rest, and on a train going to Frisco".'

'Nice work. I thought he knew Elvis?'

'One of the few people he hasn't shagged. Claims he taught him how to play the harmonica. Elvis can't deny it anyway.'

'OK, so what's the deal?'

'I've already had a chat with Jet Records. They want two hundred thousand pounds for a week's worth. I can talk to him exclusively tomorrow.'

Dick Rodger bit into the rim of his cup and dribbled coffee out of the sides of his mouth.

'We'll go with it.'

Rodger returned to scrutinising his magazine. Fiona Clamp swept back her blonde mane and strode out of the office.

Oops had arranged a private meeting with Smudger at a country hotel. They sat down to dine in a concealed corner.

'So, you should have received the first payment, Smudger.'

'Yeah, so who cares about organic melons anyway.'

'Organic melons?'

'So we've got a pretty crazy schedule ahead, uh?'

'That's right. God wants to move as quickly as possible, with the new single released the moment sales of "Treat Me like a Dog" start to dip. Then we want to record the album *tout de suite*. Luckily you guys all work pretty fast. I didn't realise that you could all read the dots, apart from Poddy. We're well ahead with planning the tour. So we're cooking with gas.'

'Speaking of working fast – is this meeting strictly business, Oops?'

'Very strictly business, Smudger. Keep it in your trousers and have another glass of wine.'

'Just checking, babe. I thought my luck was changing.'

'Well, it is. You've just got the biggest payment of your life and you've also got a big money request from *The Comet*, who want to run a serial about you.'

'Oh yeah? So what's in it for me?'

'Two hundred grand for the exclusive rights.'

Smudger's smile broadened. 'That even beats organic pomegranates.'

'Or more likely orgasmic ones in your case.'

'So what's the scene with the comic?'

'Well, their showbiz reporter, Fiona Clamp, will meet you here tomorrow afternoon. She will do an interview and run it as a series in the paper.'

'What's the chick like?'

'Well, she's very different in shape to me if that's what you want to know… and it probably is.'

Smudger nodded and smiled approvingly as Oops continued.

'She's small, with rather a large chest; in fact a very large chest. That's why they call her 'Twin Peaks'. She's about forty and blonde and probably your sort of chick, Smudger.'

'No, I go for skinny, sophisticated types like you, babe.'

Oops raised an eyebrow. 'Anyway, I need to brief you about what to say and what not to say. There are a few cats we don't want let out of the bag. But mainly Fiona wants all the stuff about you and Elvis. Did you really teach him to play harmonica?'

'Yeah, it was like an artistic exchange. He taught me to make a toasted peanut butter, banana and strawberry jam sandwich.'

'Well, that's the sort of stuff they want and it's all a great build-up to the release of the new single. That's all set, with Duke Deckster having exclusive rights to play it first.'

'He's the cat who set us on our way. "I think he did the morning show on SHAGFM" and all that.'

Oops waved her hand in front of Smudger's face to command attention.

'Right, you're clear what's going on? You meet Fiona Clamp right here tomorrow at five thirty. And strictly no stories about drugs; remarkably the Dogs have got a big following amongst schoolchildren. "Granddad rock", I think they call it.'

Smudger met Fiona promptly at the agreed time the following day and gave her a hug and a peck on the cheek as a greeting. Even the brash Fiona was taken aback. He ushered her into a corner with two large antique leather chairs.

'Take a seat here, Fiona; there's a cat coming along with a tray of coffee.'

'A cat?'

'Yeah, a waiter guy.'

'Right, OK, if we start straight away then we can have a break later.'

'Take it to the limit.'

Much to Fiona's surprise and pleasure Smudger was open, frank and matter-of-fact about his past life and loves. He was in no way evasive. They had only been talking for half an hour and got as far as the women's basketball team captain in Burbank, the aromatherapist in Beverley Hills and the colonic irrigationist in San Diego. All this, and the Elvis story still to come.

Smudger signalled to the waiter.

'Fancy a drop of red, Fiona?'

'Well, since I'm staying here and there's no worry about driving back, that would be nice.'

'Then we can get a bite to eat.'

'That's fine. It's all on me tonight.'

Fiona didn't really need to interrogate Smudger. He was very forthcoming. It was just a question of providing the occasional prompt and leaving the recorder running while he sprawled in his chair and recalled just about every story a tabloid hack could dream about, or dream about dreaming up. Smudger was dredging up affairs with a senator's wife, a Russian lap dancer and a Mexican doctor he had met in a venereal disease clinic. At times Smudger couldn't remember if he had been married five or six times. He was not in the least bit self-conscious and had no sense of shame about his past life of lusting libido.

By the time they were tucking in to a main course of grilled sea bass with a fine Chablis, Fiona had finished recording and was laughing at Smudger's stories. It was perhaps difficult to separate fact from fiction and fantasy when talking to Smudger.

'Now come on. I don't doubt you met Elvis, but did you really teach him how to play the harmonica?'

'As El would say, we can't have "suspicious minds", Fiona. El and me got on together real good. He was a really nice cat.'

'Out of all the people I've interviewed in my life, you are the most frank and completely unabashed I've ever known.'

'It's what happened. No hiding place, babe; got to be honest, I suppose. You asked the questions.'

'Didn't have to ask many.'

'This is better than organic papaya.'

'What?'

'That Chablis just hits the spot. I'll order another bottle.'

Fiona giggled. 'You know, sometimes you completely lose me.'

'Hey, I wouldn't want to lose you, babe.'

'Your CV says you're fifty-nine.'

'Well, fifty-nine-ish, give or take a couple of years. So what are you then?'

'Forty-ish.'

'That's a dangerous age when women are in their prime.'

'Dangerous for who?'

'Me.'

'You are very fit for your age, after a lifetime of decadence and debauchery.'

'I feel like a twenty-five-year old, but where can I get one at this time of night?'

Fiona giggled again. 'Would a forty-year-old do?'

'This one's strictly off the record.'

After cognac and coffee, Fiona and Smudger transferred from the lounge to her room. Both walked unsteadily, tottering down the corridor. As soon as they entered the room and locked the door, Fiona discarded her tight-fitting jacket to display the fullness of her breasts to a glassy-eyed Smudger. In a slurred voice she whispered, 'They call me 'Twin Peaks' you know, but I don't mind one little bit.'

'Heck, two big beauties. You're a great advert for the National Health Service, babe.'

'I believe you've got hidden assets too.'

Fiona and Smudger disrobed rapidly and collapsed backwards on to the bed. Fiona took the initiative and was soon straddling the contented veteran rocker and riding him vigorously, slapping him on each ear with her dangling breasts. Smudger just moaned softly. '"Hotel California". Or, as Bob Hope used to say, "Thanks for the mammaries, babe".'

Their short break over, the Dogs were summoned to a meeting at Jet Records' headquarters in Soho before going on to a recording session. Poddy, Streaky and Biffo had all arrived early and were sitting behind copies of *The Comet*. Poddy was first to break the silence.

'Jesus, have you read this bit about the nurse in Santa Monica? "We couldn't find any privacy until James pushed me into an empty operating theatre. We put on surgical masks and gowns and made love under the full lights of the operating table. It was anything but clinical".'

Biffo was perspiring.

'Blimey, he was fookin' at it with a high school gymnastics team, randy git.'

Streaky could hardly get his words out.

'Good lord, he even made love to an air hostess on Concorde.'

Poddy laughed. 'Supersonic sex!'

At that moment Smudger walked in with Oops, as the others turned over the pages and drank their coffee.

Oops turned to Smudger. 'By the way, I've had an e-mail from Fiona Clamp. She said it all went very well last night, Smudger.'

'Yes, it certainly did, I think.'

Oops addressed the group briskly.

'Now you've all read Smudger's stories, let's get to grips with our schedule. God has talked with Buddy and we all think it's worth a gamble bringing out two singles at once: "Doggone" and your revamped version of "Can I Get a Witness". One will appeal to the kids and clubbers and the other to "children of the sixties". But we expect people of all generations to buy both songs. Duke Deckster will launch both new titles on his Monday morning show. We've given him an exclusive deal on that. He's already started a big publicity campaign. We've had enough coverage to make them both take off, according to our marketing people. Then we have to stay in the studio for some sessions to rush through the album. The only break we will have is an appearance on Tuesday on the Frank Stein show. It's just you guys and that Brazilian supermodel who's going into the movies, Patricia Postura, plus that explorer git, Dan Chislehurst.'

Smudger nodded in appreciation.

'She's a little like Helen of Troy – the face that launched a thousand lines of lingerie.'

'More like the ass that launched a thousand thongs, from what I've seen,' interjected Poddy.

Oops tried to bring the meeting back to order. 'I need to get some cold showers and bromide for you, Smudger.'

Smudger's grin just widened.

Gilbert Winstanley, Godfrey Vanderbloom and Olivia Olga Ponsonby-Smart, aka the Duke, God and Oops, held a strategy meeting in an Italian restaurant in Kensington. Everything was going to plan; in fact, everything had exceeded any expectations by a very long way. Oops pointed at Duke Deckster with a breadstick.

'When you look back on this whole thing, it's amazing that you picked out that song and even more extraordinary what has happened.'

The Duke looked very thoughtful.

'Well, Olivia old girl, I just thought it was not so much catchy as infectious. I say, God, I can't wait for Monday to unleash the Dogs again. They're predicting a ten million audience at five to eight.' He broke into a parody of his radio spiel.

'The Duke gave you the lead on the Dogs. Now he's going to double dog dare you with some more canine capers from those dirty old devil dogs.'

Godfrey smiled. He was sipping an ice-cold mineral water.

'We think it's a good strategy to release the two singles together. They are a nice contrast and we think it will be a bit of a surprise. We've got blanket publicity, and all that raunchy stuff about Smudger in *The Comet* has been like manna from heaven.'

Oops hid a slight blush by picking up and perusing a printed sheet.

'Our research is incredible; it shows that the Dogs are selling right across the generations. They are a real cult thing with school kids and college students. And lots of over-sixties have even bought the CD. It's really quite unique.'

The Duke poured another glass of champagne.

'You know, I was reading *The Return of the Native* the other day and the four of them remind me of the gnarled old yokels in the village, especially the dear old boy Biffo.'

Godfrey smiled and looked at the Duke, shaking his head.

'I wouldn't use that analogy on your show, Gilbert. We're rushing through the tour with dates at ten major venues over a fortnight, starting with the NIA in Birmingham. As the man who discovered the Dogs, we would like you to do a little introduction to the concert every night. They will do a two-hour set with no support act. You OK with that?'

'Absolutely splendid, Godfrey, old chap.'

Chapter Twelve

All the TV companies had made overtures to Jet Records and squabbled like seagulls around a tip, scrapping for the rights to be first to feature the Dogs on a chat show. Olivia Olga Ponsonby-Smart and Godfrey Vanderbloom had decided to continue their policy of letting publicity seep out slowly. They wanted the old boy band to feature on a cosy chat show where they would not be subjected to heavy-duty interrogation. Their favoured option was Tuesday night's Frank Stein show. Stein was a popular London comedian and his programme came under the banner of 'family entertainment'. It was a one-hour show from eight until nine. The Dogs were to be top of the bill and joined on the set by Amazon explorer and adventurer Dan Chislehurst, plus supermodel Patricia Postura. The band had to play their new single 'Doggone' and then chat to Frank. It was simple enough. Poddy, Smudger, Streaky and Biffo were to meet at the studios, have a meal and meet Frank Stein for a briefing before the live show. They would also have several rehearsals of the song.

Two and a half hours before their chat show debut, the band sat in a spartan annexe to the staff canteen, eating rare roast beef washed down by Châteauneuf du Pape. Oops and God joined them to outline the agreed questions and lines of inquiry. So far, demand for the Dogs far exceeded supply. Their appearance was expected to treble the programme's audience to fourteen or fifteen million. Oops didn't want to leave anything to chance.

'Now look, guys, I've had a little tête-à-tête with Frank and laid down the law on a few subjects that are taboo.'

Poddy blew out his pudgy cheeks and chortled.

'Well, the main cowing taboo subject is Smudger. We'd better lock him in a closet before the show in a straightjacket and inject him with Mogadon.'

Oops smiled awkwardly. Why did she feel uncomfortable with Smudger's revelations? She recovered her composure quickly.

She was determined to sort out a corporate policy.

'We don't want this to be a sex, drugs and rock'n'roll thing. We want to make it very upbeat. Now, Frank is primed to ask you a question about your appearance on the UKTVTOP10, Biffo. You just say you were in agony with a serious back complaint and just about managed to play the drums after taking strong painkillers. Then I want the rest of you to chip in with some stuff about how brave Biffo was. But we want to gloss over that, not dwell on it. Have you got that?'

Biffo scowled and the others nodded as Oops continued her address.

'Now, we also want to run past Smudger's little stories in *The Comet* as quickly as we can. Frank has got the interview strictly on condition that he doesn't pursue certain lines. There will be just one short mention of *The Comet* series as agreed. Just give a bland answer, OK Smudger, and Frank won't follow it up. Remember, this is purely a record-selling exercise for us and that's it.'

Poddy interrupted again.

'So that's why we're not on Newsnight or Panorama.'

Oops ignored him and ran through the sort of impressions they wanted to get across, with God nodding in approval. The band listened attentively, apart from the disinterested and stern-faced Biffo, who was starting to writhe about and shift uneasily in his chair. Poddy was first to notice he was in some discomfort.

'What's the matter, old pal? Your cowing Farmer Giles aren't playing you up again?'

'Aye, I knew I shouldn't have had red wine with rare beef. It always triggers off me fookin' gout.'

Smudger smiled as always, but looked a little concerned. 'Whereabouts have you got the gout, Biffo old chap?'

'In me fookin' foot. Where do you think it is, in me fookin' arse?'

'No, of course; that's where you had the old Farmer Giles.'

'It's not fookin' funny. I'm in fookin' agony!'

Oops was both flustered and irritated.

'Look, Biffo, we rehearse in half an hour. Are you going to be OK?'

'No way. I can't hit the pedal on my bass drum; it's bloody painful.'

Smudger thought for a while.

'The guy from Def Leppard adapted to play a drum kit with one arm.'

Biffo glared at him fiercely.

'How the fook d'you expect me to learn to play the fookin' drums with one leg in half an hour, you stupid bastard.'

Streaky joined in.

'I thought you only got gout from drinking a bottle of port for breakfast.'

Oops admonished him in the manner of a haughty primary school teacher. 'That's not very helpful, Streaky, and I think you'll find the port thing is a myth.'

Poddy couldn't stop himself.

'Yeah, that's because Biffo drinks two bottles of port with his bacon and eggs.'

By now everyone was gathered around Biffo, like the crew of HMS *Victory* with the stricken Admiral Nelson. Biffo would have appreciated the historic analogy if he weren't in so much pain. He was groaning. Oops dialled a mobile number and made some inquiries. There was a return call a minute later.

'So you can get Dr Stone along to the studios soon? That would be excellent... Yes, he was the guy who saw Mr Bear before... What? You can come along in just over half an hour... That's really hunky-dory.'

The stern-faced doctor was ushered into a separate dressing room to deal with Biffo.

'So you're getting more problems with your haemorrhoids. They should have calmed down.'

'No, no, doc, I've got bloody gout. It comes on every now and then. Fookin' hurts.'

'Well, I'm going to give you a pain-killing injection now to get you through your rehearsal and another just before the show. That should see you through. What with this and piles you've certainly been through the wars.'

In the green room before the show the guests were all brought together. Biffo was silent and withdrawn and Streaky was subdued, but Poddy and Smudger were chatting effusively.

Patricia Postura entered the room clad in a tight-fitting tan leather dress with matching stack-heeled boots. She tossed back her long and lustrous black hair and looked quizzically at Smudger. Not surprisingly Smudger's eyes were transfixed on her. She waltzed up to him.

'You don't remember me, do you?'

Even Smudger looked slightly taken aback, but the smile widened to a chasm.

'I wish I could say I do.'

'That Brazilian carnival in LA about twenty years ago. I was an eighteen-year-old dancer. We all ended up in that Pink Coyote club where you were playing. We went out afterwards. Remember that midnight swim? Then we went back to your place and drank tequila.'

'Yeah, the things we do for love'.

Smudger's mind was turning over slowly, like rusting cogs in an ancient industrial machine.

'Umm. I remember now. We'll have to have a drink after the show.'

Patricia Postura smiled knowingly and nodded in agreement.

'I remember sitting and eating bananas and melons with you that morning after the carnival.'

Everyone in the room looked completely astonished by the unexpected reunion. Poddy muttered under his breath.

'Lucky jammy bastard. If he got washed up on a desert island it would be populated by page three girls and supermodels.'

Biffo's attempt at a stage whisper was as subtle as a meat cleaver.

'He must be on a fookin' drip of vitamins and Viagra.'

Biffo was uncomfortable before the show, squirming around like a sloth with cramp, but after Dr Stone had administered another jab he was able to operate the pedal on his bass drum. Frank Stein introduced his star guests with a few gags and the Dogs exploded into action. Not for the first time the director was entranced by Biffo.

'Camera two, get in close on the drummer. He's got a face like a smacked arse... He seemed decrepit and morbid in the green room, now he looks like a fiend. Camera two, get in closer on the old sod… Even tighter… Blimey, he looks out of his skull… Get in even closer… Look at his eyes… The Dogs – well, he's a dog all right, a mad dog. If he's not on drugs then I'm a Dutch drug dealer… Even tighter on two… Wow, just look at him.'

Back in the offices of *The Comet*, technicians were working diligently, processing stills of Biffo from the TV pictures. Fiona Clamp and Dick Rodger were looking intently at the images with a large, middle-aged man with dark curly grey hair and a furrowed brow. They watched the pictures very closely on a giant plasma screen. Fiona Clamp then questioned the man.

'Dr Fytch, have you seen enough to form an opinion? What do you think?'

The doctor studied another close-up of Biffo on the big screen before replying.

'From looking at those close-ups, and bearing in mind the fact that I've studied the effects of narcotics for thirty years, I would say quite conclusively that the old fellow on drums is on something like morphine. His movements, general demeanour and in particular his eyes would certainly indicate that to me.'

Dick Rodger sucked coffee from a polystyrene cup and dribbled.

'How sure are you that he's on some drug?'

'Oh, ninety-nine percent and maybe more.'

'Well, that's good enough for us,' said Dick. 'Kids are buying their records. We can't have their innocence destroyed by some druggie granddad. I've kept a big space for this one, Fiona, on page three, next to the "Breast of the Comet Page Three Corkers" competition and above the "Free alcopops for all our readers" promotion.'

The TV interview passed off with little incident. Poddy and Smudger virtually commandeered the conversation, protecting Biffo and Streaky from awkward questions. Biffo bumbled out an explanation of why he had taken medication before the first live Dogs' show. The guests retired to the Gladstone private hotel near the Westminster studios.

Biffo woke up the following morning gripped by gout and persecuted by piles. He swallowed some painkillers and staggered out of his room. At the same time Smudger exited a room across the corridor with Patricia Postura, who was wearing a tight scarlet leather catsuit that looked as though it had been sprayed on. Biffo muttered 'Fookin' 'ellfire' and then made his way down to breakfast.

Poddy and Streaky were already perusing the morning papers over a full English. Biffo sat down to join them and turned over *The Comet* to reveal a pop-eyed page three picture of him playing drums the night before. The headline said 'BACKACHE MY A★★★. HE'S A DOPED OLD DOG.'

Biffo threw the paper across the table. 'Fookin' 'ellfire.'

Chapter Thirteen

'Fook off, go on fook off and stick your fookin' heads up your fookin' arses. Just piss off and leave me in peace.' By Biffo's standards it was quite a polite response. A scrum – or 'scum', as Biffo called them – of journalists and photographers were rooting around outside his house as he returned from a walk with his stately Labradors, Lambert and Perkin.

Biffo had been born a curmudgeonly people-hater, and years of enforced contact with the species had only reinforced his prejudices. After further tabloid stories of his alleged dependency on narcotics, Biffo had been wound up to full genocide mode and was ready to do bodily harm to the sub-species of hacks besieging his house.

The only thing that stopped him was the knowledge that the resuscitation of the Dogs meant that he could afford to swap his modest suburban house for an isolated country cottage, as far away from humanity as possible. Biffo walked around the back of the house and into the kitchen. As usual Sylvia was chirpy and cheerful. In fact, her sunny outlook seemed to grow in inverse proportion to the level of Biffo's grumpiness and gloominess.

'I've just poured you out a fresh mug of tea, ducky. I'm going out with Doris at lunchtime to get some hanging baskets from the new garden centre near the abattoir.'

'Hanging baskets, hanging bastards! That's what they ought to do: hang that herd of bastards hanging around outside.'

Sylvia seemed oblivious to Biffo's outburst. 'Well, I must get going otherwise I'll be late for Doris, luvvy.'

'That's if you can get through that pack of fookin' hyenas hanging around on the pavement outside. Walking through a riot in the fookin' soup queue at Parkhurst would be nicer.'

'Oh, they'll soon be gone, love. I phoned up that nice Sergeant Kocinski and he's going to get a couple of bobbies up here to send them packing.'

'Aye, they can send them packing all right, to Angola or fookin' Afghanistan for all I care. Fookin' bastards!'

Sylvia squeezed Biffo's arm gently. 'Don't let it bother you, luvvy, just think of the money. Two brochures arrived from O'Malley, Gupta and Farquaher the estate agents this morning. There're two lovely cottages going up in Dovedale.'

Biffo grimaced and grunted, 'I'll tell you that's the only fookin' thing that's keeping me going – getting out of this place and away from those tabloid swine and those pox-ridden neighbours of ours for a bit of peace and quiet.'

Biffo started rummaging around in a pile of magazines and newspapers. 'Sylvie, have you seen that new book on The Peasants' Revolt? I couldn't find it this morning.'

'That's because you left it in the downstairs toilet. By the way, when are you off to London? Is it early tomorrow?'

'Aye, it's bastard early. Up before the fookin' lark. That's if the lark's survived all the pollution around here. Got to spend the whole day locked away doing rehearsals for the tour. Fookin' dire. I don't need any rehearsal; the others need all the fookin' practice they can get. The only one who's enjoying all the shenanigans is that sex-crazed chimpanzee, Smudger. He'd jump into bed with anything with a pulse that wears knickers. He'd shag a any creature that had an orifice.'

'Now then, ducky, when does the tour start?'

'It's a week on Friday at the National Indoor Arena in Birmingham. Apparently every ticket for the tour sold out in forty-eight hours. God only knows why. If we were playing great jazz I could understand it.'

At that moment Lambert let out a short, low growl. Biffo spun around to see a reporter and photographer in the garden. He flung open the back door as the pair scurried around to the front of the house.

'Fook off, you verminous scum. Just fook off, piss off, bugger off, sod off and arse off!'

Sylvia tried to restrain her hysterical husband. 'Look, ducky, just keep calm. After that other cheque arrived today, we can afford one of those places in Dovedale. We've just got to relax and be patient.'

Biffo screwed his face up into something that would have won a gurning competition, but was supposed to be a resigned smile. 'I suppose there's some light at the end of this fookin' endless tunnel.'

The Sancerre was slipping down nicely with fresh strawberries at the Bacon residence. The arrival of another six-figure cheque had put Arabella into a jaunty mood, and even Streaky was starting to unwind. He was wearing designer jeans, t-shirt and moccasins. Arabella was eagerly sifting through estate agents' details of luxury beachside homes in Mallorca.

'I say, Brian, this one looks a dream. Imagine inviting Cynth and Nigel over for a rubber of bridge around the poolside. This would make the Aubrey-Awstons' villa in Puerto Banus look like a hovel.'

Streaky was completely engrossed in a series of newspaper reviews of the Dogs' album.

'Hmm, listen to this: "The subtle piano style of Brian Bacon lifts this album far above mundane rock and pop. On one level the Dogs have attracted cult status, on another their music is unquestionably unique and innovative, and that's mainly down to Bacon's classical twists on the keyboards".'

The two monologues continued on independent but parallel courses.

'Here's one with a double swimming pool. I say, how delightful. A little paddling pool for the teeny-weenies and a twenty metre one for a proper swim. Si and Steph would just be green with envy.'

'What about this: "Brian Bacon's exquisite touch adds sheer class to some solid rock songs. If Rachmaninov played rock it would sound like this".'

'Oh, crikey: "An elevated lounge with windows on all four sides, with uninterrupted views out to sea and to the mountains inland". What a dandy place to slurp gin and tonic. Amelia and Archie would just love it.'

'"They call it pensioner power or crock rock but the music is sharp, fresh and enlivened by Brian Bacon's wizardry on the piano".'

'Oh, by the way, the Aubrey-Awstons have invited us to a garden party. Toby and Maudie will be there and Brigadier Mellors will be turning up with that awful frumpy woman with the hairy armpits. Squiffy and Suki are giving it a final try – they've gone for a long weekend in Worthing – and Dot and Maurice are having a big marquee in the garden for their golden do. Oh, and that new vicar up at Church Street is having an affair with the curate at St Bartholomew's.'

The pints and patter were in full supply at the Ferret and Bicycle. Despite his newly found fame, Poddy was completely unaffected. After the initial bombshell, he'd taken all the ensuing events in his stride. Anyway, he could still find a quiet corner for a beer with Little Jimmy and Big Eric. Once again the exterminator, terminator and inseminator were in session.

Eric was awestruck by *The Comet*'s revelations about Smudger's lecherous lifestyle.

'God, I remember Smudger in the fifth form. He'd shagged himself into a sodding stupor before he was sixteen.'

Poddy chuckled. 'Aye, and he's cowing well at it now, like a frog up a pump. Got to hand it to him. Or rather he hands it to anyone he can.'

Eric continued, 'I remember we went on that holiday to Mablethorpe and he would have got into the Guinness Book of Records for his weekend's score. Johnnie Mayers said to him "Don't you take any precautions?" and Smudger said, "Yeah, I never give them my name and address".'

Jimmy piped in. 'He was in the school orchestra. We had this rehearsal at seven thirty and he'd been round that Julie Poborski's place after school. He arrived at the rehearsal just as we were winding up and I asked where he'd been. He said he'd given Julie one, got a blowjob off her sister and then shagged Eva, her mum. Then the father came home and said "What have you lot been up to?" and Smudger said "Getting to know the family better". If only he'd known.'

Eric was still looking incredulously into his pint of bitter. 'Some of that stuff that's coming out in *The Comet* is just bloody amazing. I mean, it seems that no one knows, him included, how many times he's been married. He's been shacked up with that much top-class totty. Did you read yesterday about him and that woman police lieutenant in Vancouver?'

Poddy interrupted, 'Aye, they don't call them Mounted Police for nothing! Wait till you read tomorrow's. He went to see some therapist because he was addicted to sex and ended up shagging her on the couch. Then he does the business with some zoologist researching rattlesnakes and even knobs a bleedin' nun.'

Eric looked thoughtful. 'But you do wonder how much has been exaggerated and added onto the Smudger legend. Anyway, Poddy, we're all getting ready for that first concert at the NIA. Me and Jimmy will be only a few rows back. People are having to pay hundreds of pounds for tickets on the black market and we used to see you for free in the Ferret and Bicycle every week.'

'That's the price of fame, guys. I'll tell you, we've rehearsed for days on end locked away in the cowing studio with Biffo moaning about his gout and piles. I can do all the sodding songs now on automatic pilot.'

Jimmy laughed. 'I thought Biffo would be the life and soul of the party.'

'Aye, he's been about as happy as a one-legged man at an arse kicking party. But Thunderbirds are go for that first gig, any road up.'

Olivia Olga Ponsonby-Smart was sitting in the corner of an old-fashioned pub in Maida Vale sipping a glass of red wine, with another full glass lined up on the table. James 'Smudger' Smith turned a few heads as he sailed through the double doors into the saloon, attired in a brown suede cowboy hat, faded denim shirt and jeans, and brown calf-length boots. He was sporting a gold earring that almost dangled onto his shoulder.

'Hi, Oops. I see you've already got me a glass of god's own juice. So is this our first date?'

'In your dreams, you dirty old dog, especially after all I've read in *The Comet*. I've got all the schedules to go through and some extra press, radio and TV interviews I want you to fit in.'

'And I thought you would just spirit me away to your girly gaff for small talk, supper and—'

'Certainly not. The only servicing you need is with a tranquiliser dart gun three times a day. Now, Godfrey has changed a few things since that last rehearsal and we also want you to do some serious music interviews in mags and broadsheets. The album's selling like oven chips. It's students and sixth formers who are making you a cult thing.'

'What's the latest on Biffo?'

'Well, we've persevered with the brave soldier. He's had a dose of painkillers for his gout and haemorrhoids – or rather back pain.'

'Pity they couldn't help his chronic crouchiness.'

'Yes. It's a worry, but the "show must go on".'

Smudger burst into song. '"The show must go on".'

Oops battled to keep to the business agenda. 'We don't put Biffo up for interviews, so you and Poddy are very much in the frontline—'

'"You've got me, babe, living in the frontline".'

'I'm always the cue for a song, Smudger, aren't I?'

Oops was surprised to realise she felt more charmed than irritated by his interruptions. Smudger pointed at her. 'She is "something else… "'

'Gene Vincent, wasn't it?'

'C'mon now, Oops; Eddie Cochrane of course.'

'Look, quiz time over. Two of the heavy Sundays want to do massive features on you. God is keen to widen the Dogs' appeal as much as possible.'

'So how are the gigs going down?'

'Every single ticket for every single gig gone on the first day. We could have sold out several times over. This tour will be a big promo for the album. Now, there's one other change to the gigs at short notice; there'll be a support band called Nuclear Cats playing as a warm-up act. They've got a single out that's speeding up the charts, so Godfrey had the idea that they do a rapid thirty minutes before you to make it a "Dogs and Cats" tour. They're a girl band.'

'Even I'd worked that one out, Oops. I've heard of those Cats. Yeah, let me see, it's Cindy, Candy and Mandy.'

'They're the ones, and they're all forty years younger that you, so don't get any ideas.'

'"What's new pussycat… " But you're the only one for me, Oops.'

'Yes, that's what you probably told the colonic irrigationist, aromatherapist, high school gymnast, senator's wife, surgeon, mounted policewoman, sex therapist, beach attendant, zoologist, lingerie model, gossip columnist, air hostess, basketball star and—' Oops paused; 'the nun.'

Smudger pretended to look sheepish and signalled to the bar. 'Hey cat, we need some embalming fluid. Two large glasses of house red, please!'

Duke Deckster slung his briefcase to one side and sank into one of the big leather armchairs in his apartment. Juliette floated in with two champagne flutes and a vintage bottle of Pol Roger balanced on a silver tray.

'Finished the Bolly, so I've chilled a little Polly.'

Duke nodded in approval. Behind closed doors he'd already begun to shed the image of his alter ego and revert to the cultured Gilbert Winstanley. He perched his champagne on a hardback copy of *Little Dorrit* on the arm of the chair and then took a delicate sip.

'This is absolutely scrummy, old girl. The dog's bollocks, if I may. I remember once in our dorm at Eton we smuggled in some vintage champers that Barney's old man had donated. Nowhere to chill it. So we left it in a cold bath. Anyway, old Badger the housemaster found it and spanked Barney with a metal ruler. Poor boy blubbed like a little girlie.'

Juliette produced a pack of documents. 'This is your itinerary for the Dogs' tour. By the way, it's now officially the Dogs and Cats' tour. They're billing it as the biggest event since the Millennium. It seems at first glance you've got a tough schedule, but God and Oops have laid on a chauffeur to make sure you get between your radio show, PAs and the gigs.'

Gilbert put on his scholarly round spectacles. As Duke Deckster he wore contact lenses, but in private he preferred his round reading glasses.

'That's really the business. I've always said that Godfrey is a decent sort of bloke. I've already seen all the articles and various bits of bumf about the tour.'

'Yes, it's mildly astonishing; schoolchildren as young as ten have bought tickets, and there's some pensioners over sixty-five, plus that one old guy aged eighty-seven who was featured in *The Comet*. Oops told me they'd sold out every venue in double quick time and could have filled most of the places many times over. You see what you started.'

For a fleeting moment Gilbert reverted to the Duke. 'The Dogs take their bow wow wow WOW, and HOW! All thanks to the hit-maker from Kingston, Jamaica.'

In his office at *The Comet*, Dick Rodger was simultaneously drawing on a cigarette, draining a cup of coffee and drooling over topless triplets in the latest edition of *Horny Babes*. He put down the polystyrene cup and wiped away the coffee and dribble from his chin before summoning Fiona Clamp. She surged into the office like a galleon in full sail.

'Now, Fi, how's the Dogs delivery shaping up for next week?'

'Fine. I've got more Smudger revelations from a string of ex-lovers in California. There seems to be a never-ending supply. It's like cut-price baked beans. We've got some stories on the others, and we've knocked up a competition for gifts/tickets/posters and a free concert.'

Rodger picked up the empty coffee cup and bit a chunk out of the rim. 'Remind me again of the concert knick-knacks.'

'Well, we've got these blow-up miniature Zimmer frames and paper incontinence pants for the audience to throw, and just look at this...' Fiona Clamp rummaged in a file and fitted something across her face. 'It's a Biffo horror mask.'

Even Dick Rodger managed a tortured smile at the sight of the gruesome caricature.

'What about some more stuff about the hideous old git being a drug addict? We want more of that.'

'Well, the record company are trying to portray him as the wounded hero playing through the pain barrier because he's suffering from backache and gout.'

'Yeah well, fuck that, Fiona. He's just a geriatric junkie and a fucking ugly one at that. We've got all the proof we need to show he's crazed on drugs.'

81

'We're trying to get some backstage dirt from the first concert in Birmingham.'

'So they're going to get pelted with stuff as soon as they appear on stage?'

'Yeah, in every copy of Friday's *Comet* will be the blow-up Zimmer frame, incontinence pants and Biffo horror mask.'

'How are you going to get backstage after all the fallout from our stories about the old drug fiend on drums?'

'It's simple enough. I've befriended Smudger.'

Dick Rodger coughed as he inhaled his cigarette and slurped another cup of coffee. 'Seems like a lot of women have "befriended" Smudger Smith.'

Chapter Fourteen

On the morning of the first concert, Poddy and Streaky were wading into a mighty breakfast at the Hyatt Regency Hotel in Birmingham. Smudger joined them, wearing a shiny tracksuit after a workout in the gym. While Poddy and Streaky piled on huge portions of bacon, sausages and beans, Smudger carefully measured out a little fruit and cereal. The trio tucked in and sifted through a heap of the morning papers. Poddy picked up *The Comet* and a small package fell out. It was the paper's special 'doggie bag'.

'Hello, what's all this then? Hey, fellas, it's a Zimmer frame. And, bloody hell, what are these supposed to be? Incontinence pants – they'll be for you two. That's a nice touch, you've got to hand it to them. And what the cowing hell is this!'

Poddy doubled up, completely convulsed with laughter. Unable to speak, he passed the article on to Smudger, who in turn was left helpless. Streaky was similarly afflicted, reduced to a quivering stick of mirth. Poddy waved the 'Biffo horror mask' with a flourish and ceremoniously put it on. He then marched to the reception and returned with two more copies of *The Comet*.

Poddy, Smudger and Streaky were soon sitting around the breakfast table, wearing their masks, in fits of laughter and barely able to speak. Poddy was first to splutter out some words. 'Actually, this mask probably does the old boy a favour.'

Smudger chortled. 'Yes, he's probably a fair bit uglier than this. Face like a baboon's arse.'

Streaky was still sniggering. 'Yes, I have to admit it, it's really quite flattering. Some friends of Arabella call Biffo "the Zombie".'

Almost spontaneously, although Poddy was fractionally first off the mark, all three picked up a knife and fork and mimicked Biffo hammering at his drum kit. After a few moments all three were conscious of another person's presence. They peered through the slits in their masks to see Biffo glowering over the table.

'Fookin' bastards!'

Biffo then turned and angrily shuffled away. The day of the first Dogs' concert for forty-one years had got off to a bad start, and worse was to follow.

The remaining trio ordered more tea, coffee and fruit juice and continued to pore over the pile of papers. They were disturbed about ten minutes later when a flustered Olivia Olga Ponsonby-Smart and a concerned Godfrey Vanderbloom walked in. Oops almost barked at Poddy, Smudger and Streaky. 'What the hell is going on?'

God tried to maintain his customary calm. 'Look, just tell us what has happened.'

Poddy looked puzzled. 'Er, what do you mean? What's all the fuss about?'

Oops was rattled. 'Jesus, we're about to launch a multi-million pound tour and promotion, and your drummer has just walked out in a raging temper. He's pissed off in a taxi and, judging from his note, he won't be coming back.'

Smudger grinned and sighed. '"Ground control to Major Tom, your circuit's dead, there's something wrong".'

Oops was now incensed. 'You don't seem to understand this isn't a bloody silly joke. Did you upset him?'

Poddy held his hands up. 'Look, we had a bit of a laugh wearing these Biffo masks that are in *The Comet*'s doggie bag this morning. It was all in good fun, but Biffo took the 'ump and just sodded off. We thought he'd just gone back to his room.'

God intervened. 'Right, number one thing we have to do is keep the lid on this one and get Biffo to return. If we held him to contract, of course, we could sue him for millions for a start—'

God was obviously a lot more rattled than he was showing. 'Anyway, let's not talk about that; we need to find him. Why the hell won't he use a mobile? He may have gone home. We could find out from the taxi company. Poddy, I want you to go with Oops – you're the only one Biffo listens to – and persuade him to return. That's plan A.'

Streaky looked worried. 'What's plan B?'

God smiled. He was back to his smooth, unruffled self. 'There isn't one yet, Streaky. Unless you can play drums and keyboards at the same time.'

Godfrey summoned a chauffeur-driven hire car to the front of the hotel, and Poddy and Oops were sent on their tricky diplomatic peace initiative.

Smudger was lolling around in the hotel reception when three girls spilled out of a ludicrously long stretch limo and spun through the hotel lobby's revolving doors, carrying several costumes encased in polythene. He stood up, pushed back the brim of his blue suede fedora and held out a welcoming hand.

'Hey, you chicks must be Cindy, Candy and Mandy.'

The Nuclear Cats were skinny girls and broad Brummies. 'Aaawroight Smoodger!' they chorused in unison.

The Cats looked like triplets, tall, slim and blonde, with smuts of black eye make-up. Cindy ruffled the fringes of Smudger's denim shirt. 'We've read all about you.'

Smudger pretended to be taken aback. '"And the papers want to know whose shirts you wear".'

He then tried a more formal introduction. 'So you're Cindy.'

'No, I'm Candy.'

'Then you're Mandy.'

'No, I'm Cindy.'

'So I was wrong on all three counts.'

Cindy sniggered. 'After your life, it must be difficult telling one woman from another.'

Smudger comically waved an admonishing finger. 'You shouldn't believe everything you read.'

Mandy piped in, 'Well, according to *The Comet* you're the most sex-crazed man on the planet.'

'Maybe, "still crazy after all these years".'

The Cats started to check in at reception. Smudger shouted after them. 'See you all at the party after the gig.'

The three girls spun round again and yelled back all together. 'Aaawroight Smoodger!'

At that moment Smudger felt a hand squeeze his left buttock. He turned to face Fiona Clamp. She was looking at him inquisitively and pointing her breasts at him like twin rocket launchers. 'Getting to know the girls, eh Smudger? The oldest is twenty; that's forty-two years younger than your real age and even a lot younger than your fantasy age.'

'You know you're "just a babe in disguise", Fi.'

'Well, I wouldn't say that. Tell me what's going on. There's been a lot of coming and going this morning.'

'Let's hope it's more coming than going, between you and me, Fi.'

'Do you ever let up? There's something going on, isn't there? I can tell. I saw that skinny PR woman and Godfrey Vanderbloom, no less, flying around like blue-arsed flies. What was that all about?'

It was too late: Smudger engaged his mouth before his brain.

'Well, not too much really; it's just Biffo's done a runner. Got really pissed about your horror masks. Seems he's gone off in a huff – I didn't tell you that.'

'No, of course you didn't. So they've gone off to find the cadaverous old bastard and bring him back?'

'Yeah, and if they find him they'll be "walking back to happiness".'

'Give it a rest with the song titles, Smudger. What will you do if he refuses?'

'God only knows.'

Fi grimaced. 'Thanks, Smudger, you've been a big help.'

'I think I'm due payment for that.'

'The only payment I'll make for you is the vet's bill to get you neutered. That's the only way to protect the girls in Nuclear Cats, although judging from what I hear even you might find them a bit too hot to handle.'

'Naah. You know me – I'm "addicted to love".'

'See you at the party, big boy.'

Poddy and Oops burst out of a big black limo outside Biffo's neat suburban semi in Derby. No hacks were to be seen: they'd followed the Dogs to Birmingham. As they hustled up the garden path, Lambert and Perkin barked, and Sylvia peered through the curtains before rushing to open the front door. She looked perplexed.

'What's the matter?'

Poddy put his hands up and spoke calmly.

'Is Biffo here?'

Sylvia looked alarmed. 'Why, of course not. He's with you. I spoke to him last night at the hotel in Birmingham after you'd had a rehearsal and sound check.'

Poddy blew out his cheeks and thought for a moment. 'OK, I know. Nothing to worry about, Sylv, I promise you. I know exactly where he'll be. Let's get going.'

Poddy ushered Oops back to the car, leaving Sylvia rooted to the spot on the garden path. In the limo Oops gesticulated to Poddy with the open palms of her hand, demanding an explanation.

'What now then?'

'The Goat.'

'The Goat?'

'The One-Horned Goat.'

'What?'

'The cowing One-Horned sodding Goat.'

'What's that, for Christ's sake?'

'It's a wayside pub up in the Derbyshire hills that Biffo goes to for the occasional break when he's fed up with the world.'

Oops gave a sarcastic laugh. 'That's most of the time, or in fact all of the time, isn't it?'

'Well, Biffo is very much a man of few habits, and few friends. But he always goes up to The Goat. It's a fair trek, but an old teaching mate of Biffo's runs the place. One of the select band of friends he's cowing well got. It's the sort of place bearded hikers in outsize anoraks go to eat their cheese sarnies, and reclusive, sad old gits like Biffo hang out there too.'

'Well, I hope you're right.'

'Ninety-nine percent certain.'

'How long will it take to get to this One-Legged Goat?'

'One-*horned*. Best part of an hour.'

Biffo lurched wearily towards the inn, giving the impression of a man wading through porridge. He couldn't help noticing, as he approached, that his beloved old Goat appeared quite unfamiliar. For a start there was a large new tarmac car park instead of a muddy field criss-crossed with tyre tracks. The frontage of the old hostelry had been spruced up, and to one side was a huge new extension and conservatory.

Biffo snorted, stared up at a bold new sign and read out aloud:

'"The One-Horned Goat – Hotel and Conference Centre". Fookin' conference fookin' centre.'

Biffo walked into the bright new interior. The middle of the old inn had been completely gutted and renovated. Biffo shuffled suspiciously towards a long, modern bar. A man in a smart black three-piece suit and white shirt pulled out a clipboard. 'Good afternoon, sir. Which party are you with?'

'Party, what do you mean party?'

'Well, today it's the Young Conservatives economic study group, Advertising, Image and Media's training course, and Atkins' Surgical Goods' marketing conference.'

Biffo looked disorientated and dismayed.

'Where's Jonjo?'

'Jonjo?'

'Yeah, Jonjo O'Casey.'

'Oh, Mr O'Casey sold out ten months ago and since then we've developed this place into Britain's first business retreat. Took a lot of work. The old place was rotting, rusting and falling to bits. We did it all top to tail in about nine months.'

Biffo was struck dumb.

The man in the black three-piece pointed at the gleaming taps on the bar. 'We are open to the non-conference trade, too, if you'd like a drink.'

Biffo spluttered out between clenched teeth, 'Aye, well in that case, I'll have a pint of Sow's Grunt.'

'Sow's Grunt… No, doesn't ring a bell. Sorry. We've got Smallpiece draught, and Winkelstein and Blewett's premium lager.'

'Fookin' chemical muck. I'd rather sup my own fookin' piss.'

'Sir, you're welcome to a drink, but I think it would be better if you go into the Small Business bar, as the Young Conservatives study group are due a break in here at any moment.'

'Wanky beer and fookin' Young Conservatives. This used to be a nice watering hole. Now it's a nasty fookin' hellhole.'

'Now sir, there's no need to get abusive.'

'Look, I'll have a pint of that shit stuff and sit in your fookin' business bastard bar or whatever you call it, if you order me a fookin' taxi to get the hell out of here.'

'Of course, sir. That'll be three pounds fifty for the beer.'
'Three fookin' pounds fookin' fifty!'

Several miles away in the black limo, Poddy received a call on his mobile. He gave a thumbs-up to Oops.

'OK, as we suspected, the taxi company that collected Biffo from the hotel have confirmed they took the old buzzard straight to the One-Horned Goat. So the old git's at the Old Goat.'

Oops looked relieved. 'Now you've got the job of persuading him to return. I believe God is looking for a stand-in drummer, just in case, and is going to claim that Biffo was too sick to perform. He's even talked about paying him off and getting in another geriatric drummer boy.'

'Well, you can't cowing well do that. I suppose that's sodding plan B, but what you don't realise is that Biffo's style is completely unique, unfortunately. It's a jazz technique with complicated sequences. You could easily find a stand-in for me or Smudger, but to find someone to play like Biffo or Streaky would be as difficult as finding a virgin in Birmingham's Broad Street on a Friday night. Leave it with me; I'll sort it out.'

After a long journey and several wrong turns, the imposing black automobile drew up outside The One-Horned Goat Hotel and Conference Centre. Oops signalled for Poddy to go in.

'You take on this mission on your own. You're the only person he ever listens to.'

'OK, here goes. He'll be in a little room at the back with his nose dripping into a pint of bitter.'

It was Poddy's turn to be astounded by the face-lift to the remote inn. He walked around the building twice before peering in through a side window. His gaze homed in on a forlorn figure sipping a drink as though he was sampling some nasty cough mixture. Poddy had always been a good 'people person'. His intuitive social skills had helped him to build up his pest control business. He decided on some drastic action. There was a side door through to the Small Business bar. Biffo crept in as quietly as a furtive ghost in carpet slippers. He enveloped Biffo in a bear hug and kissed him on his bald pate.

'Come on, old fella, we're going back. You can't say no to a fortune for yourself and the others, no matter what. For Sylvie's sake – you can soon buy any property you like up here.'

Biffo shrugged, but looked a little brighter. A few minutes later he was sitting in the back of the big black limo with Poddy and Oops, heading back to Birmingham.

Chapter Fifteen

The streets were thronged with people of all ages, some waving inflatable Zimmer frames and others wearing *The Comet*'s Biffo masks. Many girls – and even some men – wore T-shirts boasting 'I'VE SLEPT WITH SMUDGER'. The older fans, in a sort of ageist one-upmanship, had their own slogan: 'I SLEPT WITH SMUDGER THE YEAR JFK WAS SHOT'.

It was like a street carnival around Birmingham's National Indoor Arena. It wasn't just 'pensioner power' that had arrived. The clever double-billing of Dogs and Cats had attracted not only the old but everyone from pre-pubescent kids to veterans in their sixties. Thirty-five-pound tickets for the concert were changing hands for ten times that amount. Touts were loving it. Dogs T-shirts, posters and souvenirs moved faster than an octogenarian on pension day. Even large portraits of Biffo in his vest and pants taken from *The Comet*'s front-page picture were selling for a fiver a time.

Groups of well-oiled students gathered around the bars chanting the chorus from 'Treat Me like a Dog', now Britain's biggest-selling single of all time.

> *Cos you treat me like a dog*
> *Treat me like a dog*
> *You've got me yelping and a yapping, snarling and a snapping*
> *Cos you treat me like a dog*

The words echoed round the hundreds of Dogs fans swarming outside the NIA. It was like the build-up to a football match without the rivalry – after all, everyone was supporting the same team. Coaches had arrived from all over the country. As well as a huge press presence from all over the world, the audience was going to be studded with stars and celebrities. Nuclear Cats were set to open the show with a short set of little more than half an hour – enough to exhaust their repertoire. There would then be a short break before Duke Deckster welcomed the Dogs on stage at about a quarter to nine.

James 'Smudger' Smith was talking to three of the road crew in the corridor outside the Dogs' dressing room as the Nuclear Cats glided past to take the stage. They were wearing fake tans and very little else. A flash of something gold and sparkly, micromesh, backless mini dresses with plunging necklines and soaring hemlines on bronzed, taut young bodies. They clipped along on stiletto, diamante-studded sling-backs.

'Aaawrooight Smoodger!'

'Best of luck, Mandy.'

'I'm Candy.'

Smudger smiled fondly as the girls strutted sexily up the passageway, leaving behind a warm fug of cheap perfume and hairspray. Smudger turned and winked at the roadies.

'"She was just seventeen". Hot chicks, huh!'

After weeks on the road with the girls, the roadies were immune to their obvious sensuality and hardly reacted. One of the crew looked at his watch.

'An hour to go, Smudger. Don't you feel a little bit nervous?'

'A bit, but not when I'm out there with my trusty bass. Reminds me of a concert in Frisco with the Doors. Jim Morrison called me up and asked me to join them for a few gigs. Life in the fast lane all right. At the time I was doing a few sets with Crosby, Stills, Nash and Young. I turned down the chance of calling it Crosby, Stills, Nash, Young and Smith. Those cats really wanted me on board.'

He smiled at the memory. 'Jesus, they must have been on something special to want me around. Anyway, at the time they were based in LA, and I had this hot chick in New York. Then I started doing some studio stuff with BB King and Muddy Waters. It was all kinda "Lucy in the Sky with Diamonds". One big gig, one big jam, one big session and lots of heavy stuff, man.'

The roadies hadn't got a clue what he was going on about but nodded politely. The willowy Oops tripped down the corridor in mother hen mode. Smudger greeted her with a hug. '"Let's spend the night together".'

Oops gave him a professional smile. 'Sorry, Smudger, I think we're all much too busy for that. Now how's Biffo?'

'Well, for him, pretty cool. He's sort of matter-of-fact and miserable rather than morose. Must have had some happy pills.'

'Where is he?'

'He's chilling out. Poddy has taken him under his wing. They're sharing tea and chocolate biscuits.'

'And what about Streaky?'

'When I last saw him he had just three clues to go in *The Times* crossword.'

Oops smiled happily at Smudger. It was all going well.

'You look an absolute babe when you do that, bad for an old guy's blood pressure.'

Oops quickly returned to matters in hand.

'So everything looks tickety-boo.'

'My life could only be tickety-boo if I spent it with you, Oops.'

'If you're a good dog tonight we might share a glass of cooking red at the reception afterwards.'

'I'll take that as a date, babe.'

The heavy clack of sharp heels on the tiled corridor floor made everyone turn around. Fiona Clamp was striding towards them, her nipples protruding through a skimpy white blouse, pointing the way ahead. Oops glared in her general direction.

'No press allowed down here. You're restricted to the media box and the press conference afterwards.'

'Twin Peaks' shrugged dismissively.

'I've been given an official backstage pass actually, so I can go exactly where I like.'

Oops was furious. 'How did you get that?'

Fiona slid her eyes in Smudger's direction. Oops followed her gaze. Smudger couldn't mask his guilt: he looked like someone caught with his fingers in the till. Oops shook her head slowly in despair as he slunk back into the dressing room, closely followed by a smug Fiona.

Inside, Biffo sat in a corner dressed in a threadbare, tea-stained vest and old Y-fronts, clutching a mug which was steaming up his horn-rimmed glasses. He was wearing a sock on his right foot with his big toe pushing through a large hole; his left foot was red and swollen with gout. Like a gunslinger on the draw, Fiona Clamp whipped out a small digital camera from her bag and fired off a succession of shots. Biffo wiped the steam from the hot tea off his glasses.

'Who the fook let you in, you fookin' cow. Now fookin' well fook off out of my fookin dressing room.'

'It's not your dressing room, it's Birmingham City Council's actually,' said Fiona with a grin. She just managed to get out of the door before a mug of scalding tea hit the wall and exploded into small shards of ceramic shrapnel.

'Fook off!'

Twin Peaks scuttled off down the corridor, grinning, her quarry captured in the camera she clutched to her breasts.

Back in the dressing room a doctor had turned up. It was a bit like the prelude to a top football match: the medico had to carry out a late fitness test on Biffo. He administered painkillers for his gout and quizzed him about the state of his piles. Oops decided that this was the moment to leave. Poddy was trying hard to keep Biffo's spirits up.

'Don't worry, old mate, you look like every woman's nightmare. Did you get that vest and pants from Army and Navy or Oxfam? I had a pair like that when I was about twelve. Come to think of it…'

His sentence was cut short by a shout from Streaky. 'The raptor is a wizard! That's it – I can't believe I didn't get that straightaway. After all it's so simple. A raptor is a bird of prey. Merlin is a wizard and a bird of prey. I've beaten my record, done *The Times* crossword in seventeen minutes.'

Poddy slapped him on the back.

'Well done, mate, but that's cowing nothing. I've done *The Comet* teatime puzzle in ten minutes, in between catching a squirrel in a loft and ridding a shed of a rats' nest.'

Streaky ignored him and, in good humour, moved over to a small electric piano and started to limber up on the keyboards. Smudger sat down and unpeeled a large green banana, tapping his foot in time to Streaky's playing. Biffo, still dressed in his tatty underwear, was breathing heavily on his glasses and wiping them on his vest, which was now covered with fresh splashes of tea from the mug he'd thrown at Fiona Clamp.

The dressing room door flew open and Duke Deckster – or rather Gilbert Winstanley – marched in theatrically.

'I say, chaps, just about twenty minutes to go until the first over from the pavilion end. The girls are going down a storm. Not surprising really in those outfits.' A pause, as he stared at Biffo. 'Your outfit is pretty chic, old boy. I say, is there some tea left in that pot?'

Biffo grunted. Gilbert Winstanley's accent and breeding grated. Biffo was a class warrior and Gilbert's type was the enemy. 'Aye, there fookin' is and you can pour it yourself, or didn't they teach you that at fookin' Eton?'

Gilbert Winstanley chuckled. 'Taught us more than that, like how to blend a fine Darjeeling with Kenyan and Assam... But if my taste buds are telling me correctly, this is more like supermarket economy tea bags, about five hundred to a sack. But it does the job of lubricating the old tonsils. Right, I'm off, got to get into my glad rags to introduce you chaps.'

'Fook off then,' said Biffo 'and take your fookin' airs and graces with you.'

Smudger pushed up the brim of his brown suede hat.

'Fifteen minutes to go. "Take your protein pills and put your helmet on".'

The Cats had wound up the crowd, and now the first Dogs' show for over forty years was about to get underway. Duke Deckster had taken over from his alter ego Gilbert Winstanley and stood spotlit on the dark stage, rapping out an introduction. The crowd roared, the stage lit up, and the band exploded into action in a blaze of smoke, lights and colour, as a hail of rubber Zimmer frames, incontinence pants, plastic walking sticks, vests and vitamin pills rained onto the set. The Dogs tore straight into some old blues standards. Poddy was simply inspired. He seized the moment and looked almost jubilant, his gravelly voice filling the vast arena. Smudger was wreathed in smiles. Streaky, with his silver hair, usually cropped short every three weeks, now overflowing onto his collar, had lost all his inhibitions and was embracing his new-found stardom at last. Biffo snarled and sneered – even more so when the Dogs launched into 'Treat Me like a Dog' and that vocal loop of his famous rant that was mixed into the song. The intro to their big hit prompted another massive bombardment of Zimmers and plastic pants.

For most of the ninety-minute gig the crowd stood, stamped, clapped, danced and propelled the contents of *The Comet*'s doggy bags towards the stage. Once into their stride, the hours of rehearsal paid dividends for the Dogs. The tour had got off to a spectacular start. The Dogs were on heat.

Back in the dressing room, Poddy and Biffo slugged from bottles of Marston's Pedigree, shunning a fridge full of ice-cold Budweiser in favour of their traditional, warm brown bitter. Poddy set down his bottle with a satisfied sigh.

'There you go, old fella. That wasn't so bad. You'll soon have that place up in the Dales, and all the surplus sets of cowing vest and pants that the Army and Navy store can muster.'

'Aye, well, after playing top-class jazz for forty-odd fookin' years, this stuff is kids' play, bloody shite.'

Smudger gulped a large glass of red wine.

'Phew guys, "it's only rock'n'roll t". Brian Bacon, you were the hottest cat on the hottest keyboards. OK, so where's the party, huh?'

The dressing room door was flung open and Oops, God and Duke Deckster swept in. Oops looked overjoyed, her cheeks flushed and eyes shining. Amidst the loose maul of hugs, huddles, cuddles and high fives, Oops threw her arms around Biffo and kissed him on both cheeks. For the first time in months Biffo beamed.

Smudger saw her bright-eyed excitement and felt a pang of jealousy.

'What about me, babe!'

But Oops had recovered her composure and, remembering the 'Twin Peaks' moment, chose to ignore him. Smudger pretended it didn't bother him.

Oops clapped her hands. 'Now, guys, we've got to do the presser – right now!' Her shout got their attention. 'Those nice people from Grub Street need their stories, so come on! I've told them it's a ten-minute gang bang.' She paused, expecting and getting a chorus of jeers, before smiling and continuing. 'You know what I mean: no one-on-one interviews. As soon as it's all over, there's a party laid on in the Lon Chaney Suite.' More cheers. Oops grinned indulgently. This was how it should be. No problems, everyone loving everyone else.

The party was restricted to the Dogs, the Cats and their entourage of roadies and technicians, the executives of Jet Records, plus assorted wives, husbands and partners.

Owing to demand the tour had been increased to three weeks, with seven more concerts at various large venues around Britain. The next gig was at the Drill Hall in Pugworthy, the biggest venue in Britain. But there was a day's break before that, and the Dogs were determined to enjoy their night.

Poddy had really seized the moment at the National Indoor Arena. He was holding court, entertaining his family, Barbara, Buddy, Bonny and Biffo.

'Told you we'd be back, but I didn't think it would take forty-one cowing years. Just done it a few days before I get the bus pass. Not so much a comeback, more "where the hell did they come from". We're not the new kids on the block, more like old gits in shock.'

Even Biffo laughed aloud at that one. He felt a little more at ease now. He could relax a bit with Poddy and his family. Buddy pulled his father to one side.

'I've renegotiated the tour deal. Just check it and get all the lads to sign.'

'OK. No need to check, just get it done, son.'

Duke Deckster swaggered across, holding hands with Juliette.

'Stonking good show, chaps, really top drawer.'

One of the nearby roadies overheard Duke and turned to a mate.

'Blimey, that Duke Deckster does a great fucking impression of an upper-class twit.'

Streaky was trapped in a corner by an excited Arabella.

'I've seen these most fantastic sofas at Newbold and Crumps with the most darling tasselled cushions…'

Her words bounced off a dazed Streaky.

'I was quite pleased, but I think I rushed that first solo in "I'll be Doggone"…'

'They've got some marvellous new fridges in Stillwells. I just love those dandy ice-making machines…'

'I think we are surprisingly tight and disciplined as a combo. Poddy does really drive the band from the front. He's actually got a great voice, could have been an operatic tenor…'

'Those kitchen plasma screens are going at half price in Arbuthnot and Small. We could really do with one…'

'It's extraordinary how that keyboard I'm playing can replicate a grand piano. A few months ago I would never have believed it…'

'By the way, Maurice and Dot say that the new all-weather garden furniture at Fornswaters is excellent value. It's not even damaged by snow and ice…'

'It never really struck me before, but Smudger is a really top-notch musician. He really holds everything together.'

That stopped Arabella in her tracks. Her virtual tour around various department stores was brought to an abrupt halt. In fact, she nearly choked on a mushroom vol-au-vent.

'There's only one thing that sex-crazed chimp has a talent for, and he's at it again, sniffing around those pitiful young girls who did that sort of amateur talent show before you came on.'

Even that failed to penetrate Streaky's reverie about his performance. He stared wistfully into the distance.

By midnight the party was virtually over. Biffo, Poddy and Streaky had long since gone to their rooms. There were four people left around a table playing 'pass the parcel' with a bottle of red wine – Cindy, Candy, Mandy and Smudger. Three young kittens and one old dog, who was feeling more like a cat that had got the cream.

Cindy, Candy and Mandy all drained a glass in one and yelled out in unison.

'Aaawroight Smoodger!'

They then refilled their glasses and downed them without a breath.

Smudger eased back the brim of his hat.

'Time to slide inside the old sleeping bag before hitting the trail again in the morning, but there's a vintage bottle of claret in my room. C'mon chicks, I mean cats, come and share a glass with me.'

The Cats sniggered and repeated their Brummie harmony.

'Aaaaaawwroooight Smooooodger!'

Cindy pulled the hat down over his eyes.

'But just one glass and no rumpy-pumpy. We've read about you.'

'And at your age, too,' chimed in Mandy.

Candy slurred, 'And there's one thing we want to see.'

The four staggered, tripped and tottered into a lift, re-emerged on the top floor of the hotel and fell into Smudger's penthouse suite. Smudger popped the cork on a bottle of Château Margaux and poured out four large glasses. He then slid open a drawer in his bedside cabinet and produced a six-inch-long, ready-rolled joint.

'You chicks familiar with these?'

Cindy yawned. 'Yeah, course. Used to smoke them behind the gym at school in Small Heath.'

Mandy butted in. 'Yeah, and much bigger than that, an' all.'

They sat on Smudger's king-size bed, passing the wine bottle clockwise and the joint in the opposite direction. Smudger took a deep drag on the spliff and handed it to Cindy. Candy necked a large glass of wine and half-whispered, 'We want to see your famous instrument.'

Smudger replied, 'What, my vintage Fender bass that Jimi Hendrix used in recording sessions?'

'No, we mean your *big* instrument,'

Mandy cut in, 'Yes, we mean your *really* big instrument.'

Smudger looked pissed, stoned and puzzled.

'You've lost me, cats, I mean chicks.'

The Cats then started to amplify their request.

'Your todger!'

'We've read about it in *The Comet*.'

'Yeah, let's see it.'

'C'mon, just give us a peep.'

'Yeah, wanna see it, your nudger.'

'They say it would get on Record Breakers.'

'C'mon, Smudger, just give us a private viewing.'

'Yeah, get your willy out for the lasses.'

'Show us your John Thomas, Smudger.'

For probably the first time in his life, Smudger felt a little embarrassed.

'Hey chicks, I mean Cats, just a quick flash for fun. I can't believe I'm doing this – and no taking pictures with your mobile phone.'

Smudger handed the joint to Candy, stood ceremoniously in the centre of the bedroom and dropped his jeans and boxers to the floor. The Nuclear Cats yelped, cheered and applauded.

'Jeez, it's like a baby's arm.'

'More like a bloody gorilla's arm.'

'It's a fucking monster.'

'It's four times bigger than Rampant Rabbit.'

'It's as big as me granddad's prize marrow.'

'Remember Mickey "Meat" O'Malley in 5C? We thought he was hung like a donkey, but his was half the size of Smudger's.'

'So Smudger, that's why old men wear big baggy trousers. It's like looking at those big sausages on the deli counter at Saino's.'

Smudger pulled up his pants again and they continued the weed and wine party. Cindy was first to succumb, collapsing back on the bed and falling into a deep sleep. Candy, Mandy and Smudger followed suit quickly, Smudger passing out in a crumpled heap at the foot of the bed.

Inside a large broom cupboard just two doors down the corridor, Fiona Clamp and Darren Spivey were holed up, waiting for the outcome of the grass and grog party.

Spivey was uncomfortable and impatient. 'Sodding hell, Fi, why the fuck are we holed up in here and not in a proper room?'

Fiona Clamp spat at him like a striking cobra. 'Because they're all taken, you whingeing git.'

'So, I'm pressed up against you in this cupboard for the night with ham and tomato sandwiches and a flask of coffee? You could at least give me a blowjob to pass away the time.'

They'd already been cramped in the cupboard on the top floor of the hotel for three hours. Darren Spivey was getting more and more edgy.

'Look, just stay cool, Darren. I got this morning's big front-page Dog scoop with Biffo in his vest and pants.'

'Yeah, that should make about half of Britain throw up their coffee and cornflakes.'

'Well, Daz, we've got another front-page special – Smudger and Nuclear Cats having a little four-in-a-bed session.'

'How do you know for sure they're all in his room?'

'I've been keeping a close watch all evening. Unless one or more have clambered down the fire escape, they're all in there, OK?'

'So what the fuck do we do?'

'Well, if they come out one by one that's OK; we can do a sequence of shots. After, all they're coming out of the same room. But if they break out together then it's a fucking belter.'

Despite their discomfort, Fiona and Darren finally fell asleep in the cupboard. It was Fiona who awoke with a start and rubbed her neck as she looked at her watch. She turned and elbowed the photographer in the ribs. 'Daz, for Christ's sake wake up! It's half past seven.'

'Oh Jesus, I feel like I've been run over by a JCB. They haven't left the fucking room, have they?'

'No, I'm sure they haven't. Let's get ready to rock and roll.'

It couldn't have worked better for *The Comet*'s super-sleaze team. The three Cats and Smudger all awoke about the same time, drowsy, disorientated and fully clothed, and decided to go for breakfast. The four walked out of the room together, holding hands in jaunty fashion, and walked straight into a barrage of flashbulbs. Smudger theatrically played to the camera as Darren Spivey fired off a volley of shots.

The next morning *Comet* Editor Dick Rodger was nervously excited. The exclusive pictures of Biffo in his threadbare and grubby vest and pants had featured on the front page and in a 'page three special'. That morning's edition displayed a smug Smudger and three startled Cats emerging from a hotel room holding hands. The headline said 'Four-in-a-bed romp', with a caption: 'Old Dog proves he's the Cat's whiskers'. There was also a centrefold spread titled 'Old Dog teaches Cats new tricks'.

Dick Rodger sucked on a cigarette and slurped from his coffee, gripping both the fag end and polystyrene cup in his right hand. 'The managing director is delighted. The circulation figures for the last few days, what with the doggy bag and picture of that dirty old git in his pants, have set a record. Now we've got the best picture story of the lot today. This Dogs' story has been like gold dust to *The Comet*, and you've been on the case from the word go, Fi.'

He tried to catch her eye, but Fiona Clamp was wearing a push-up bra and he couldn't lift his eyes above chest level. She chortled as she looked at the paper. 'And you'd never believe it, that randy old git claims they just had a party in the room, fell asleep and never even took their clothes off. Maybe they all still believe in Father Christmas.'

Dick Rodger wiped away a dribble of coffee with his sleeve. 'If anybody believes that then Adam never shagged Eve.'

Dick Rodger sidled over to his desk and put the paper down next to the latest *Horny Babes* magazine, which was opened up on the middle page spread. 'Fiona, I want you to stick with the rest of the Dogs tour. Where are they next?'

'Well, after a day's break they're at the Drill Hall, Pugworthy, tomorrow night.'

'Serve 'em bloody well right. If Britain had a septic boil it would be Pugworthy. Fucking dump!'

'The hall's that converted RAF hangar. It's bloody vast. It holds fifteen thousand.'

'Well, Fi, we'll leave it to you. Our readers can't get enough of this stuff. Stick to it like a leach. Smother them,' he added, staring at her enormous breasts.

Fiona Clamp turned from his gaze and tottered out of the room on her six-inch heels. Dick Rodger sighed and resumed his perusal of *Horny Babes*.

Chapter Sixteen

After the success of the first gig, the mood in the Dogs' camp as their second date drew near was more relaxed. Dr Chris Stone had now been engaged as a permanent member of the tour to pander to Biffo's needs. The ravages of piles and gout had returned, and Biffo needed medication to get through every concert. The doc also helped by bearing the brunt of the sixty-seven-year-old drummer's incessant whining and moaning. Poddy was content, Smudger in a daze and Streaky starting to revel in his unexpected fame. All four were in the dressing room before the concert along with Buddy Peabody, Oops and Duke Deckster. Suddenly they heard a succession of screams and yells from the room next door.

Biffo had just swallowed two painkillers. 'What the fookin' 'ellfire was that?'

Cindy, Candy and Mandy burst in. Mandy just managed to blurt some words out. 'Oh, my god, it's horrid, get someone.'

Poddy was first to react. 'Hey, kids, calm down. What's the cowing problem?'

Cindy stammered out, 'There's a rat in our dressing room. It's massive.'

Poddy put his finger on his nose and Streaky smiled. 'Looks like a job for you.'

Poddy walked out and into the next-door dressing room. Two of the roadies watched as he got down on all fours and started crawling around the floor, making strange squeaking noises and breathing out very deliberately. Five minutes later, Poddy emerged from the dressing room carrying a big, brown rat by the tail. He walked to the nearest fire door and burst the bars open. Setting the rat gently on the ground outside, Poddy flicked his fingers loudly. The rat regained consciousness and scuttled off.

Poddy had been completely unaware that the door was adjacent to a queue of fans waiting to get into the Drill Hall. They looked on in amazement as the frontman of the world's biggest-selling rock band walked out carrying what looked like a dead rat by the tail and then seemed to bring it back to life. The two roadies were amazed. 'What did you do, for fuck's sake?'

'Years of cowing experience.'

'What as?'

'I've got a business as a rat catcher.'

'Yeah, right.'

'All I did was hypnotise the rat using my eyes and by breathing down its nostrils. I then dumped it outside and brought it out of a deep sleep and back to consciousness.'

Poddy strode back into the dressing room. 'OK, crisis over. Roland Rat's done a runner.'

Duke Deckster introduced the Dogs that evening on stage by announcing that the crumbling combo had not only made it one, two and three in the charts in Britain, they'd also done the same with the release of their three singles in America. If anything the gig was even more successful than the first night at the NIA. Buddy Peabody called a post-gig meeting with the band in the dressing room.

'Look, I've had a long meeting with Godfrey Vanderbloom and some of the top exec guys from Jet Records. I've negotiated a new contract that you all need to agree and sign. Honestly, it's a fantastic deal.'

Biffo interrupted, 'Aye, well what's in the fookin' bastard deal then?'

Poddy stroked the top of Biffo's bald pate. 'Come on, old chap, be a bit patient; let the boy speak.'

Buddy resumed. 'They want a deal for a tour of the States, followed by another big British and European tour, and two more albums. With all the bonuses and everything else involved, the whole package should be worth – wait for it – £20 million each.'

Poddy whistled aloud. 'Aye, that's great, Biffo. You can piss off to Marks and Sparks for your new vests and pants now. You'll be able to pay out more in alimony and paternity suits, Smudger, and Arabella will be able to spend all your dough on new settees and cushions, Streaky. I might buy a cowboy outfit myself, maybe Derby County!'

Buddy continued. 'The draft of the new contract is with the lawyers. We've still got the deal for the first album, current singles and this tour. You all need to read through the small print for yourselves, but I don't think there're any grenades thrown in. It's all pretty straightforward and the £20 million is almost like a minimum payment.'

Biffo sneered, 'I'll fookin' believe it when we get our hands on the dough. It'll make all these shenanigans worthwhile. Then I can get back to playing some proper music.'

Streaky held up both hands. 'Come on, Biffo, you've got very little to grumble about. This must be beyond your wildest dreams. What's the matter with you? You've already had the best part of a million. It's better than teaching 3C History. Just be a little grateful. Buddy's done a great job sorting out these contracts.'

Smudger mused, 'Yeah, grateful. That reminds me of a gig I did with the Grateful Dead in Sacramento. We did a sort of impromptu set in this cellar bar. Played a sixteen-minute improvisation with Jerry Garcia...'

Biffo broke in, 'Jerry fookin' Garcia! He's fookin' snuffed it as well. Is there anybody alive who you worked with? Dead men can't tell any fookin' tales.'

Poddy calmed everybody down and brought them back to the matter in hand. 'Look, I can't believe this. We should be whooping it up and celebrating. It's a fantastic deal. This is what we've always wanted. Well, I tell you it's what I've always cowing well wanted, apart that is from two new strikers, a couple of centre backs a goalie and a midfield player for Derby County.'

Later that night, the Dogs' tour entourage held a relaxed gathering at Pugworthy's only starred hotel, the Rex. Smudger was sitting in a corner of the bar talking to Streaky, when two well-preserved, bold and brassy women joined them on the settees. The first woman tapped Smudger on the knee. 'You don't remember me, do you?'

Smudger sang, '"It started with a kiss…"'

The woman looked puzzled.

'Hot Chocolate – you do remember me! It started with a kiss.'

'But do you remember me?'

'No, I don't believe I do, babe,' conceded Smudger.

'We were on your first tour, me and my pal here, Roxanne.'

Smudger just screeched out 'Roxanne' and vigorously strummed out some imaginary chords.

'We followed you all over the country and went to every gig. I've still got your first album on vinyl. I'm Anne Slot. You must remember me and Roxanne. You know: the Hammersmith Palais, and Baileys at Leicester, and the Rickytick at Windsor...'

Smudger sank back in his seat and pondered a while. 'Yeah, I vaguely remember a few of those gigs.'

'Do you remember what you used to call me?'

'No, no not exactly.'

'You used to call me Anne of a Thousand Ways. We followed your whole tour and now we're back. If you're the geriatric mega-stars, we're the geriatric groupies.'

Streaky looked on disapprovingly before turning to talk to Buddy Peabody, who was enjoying a bottle of strong lager. Smudger was left chatting to the two ageing fans. Roxanne was silent, Anne was garrulous. The Dogs' bass player was soon engrossed in their company and enjoying a fine Châteauneuf du Pape.

Fiona Clamp had managed to latch onto Duke Deckster – an old friend who owed her plenty of favours – in order to gain admission to the party, to the annoyance of Olivia Olga Ponsonby-Smart. *The Comet* columnist watched from a distance as Smudger chatted animatedly to the two old tarts. Surely there wasn't another big picture scoop on the way? 'The old Dog and two ancient bitches on heat'.

The gathering gradually thinned, leaving Smudger, Anne and Roxanne cocooned together in a corner. Smudger was in jocular mood. 'I'm on the road again. I'll tell you something, though: you two chicks still look cool.'

Once again Anne spoke and Roxanne stayed silent. 'Well, we were just seventeen...'

Smudger couldn't resist interrupting. '"That sort of rings a loud bell in my music and song-writing career". If my memory serves me correctly I helped John and Paul write something like that.'

'No, we were both just seventeen when we followed you on the tour. I'd just left school and got a job with the Co-op, and Rox worked at Norah's knitwear factory. We were so sad when you broke up, weren't we, Rox?'

Roxanne nodded in agreement and Anne continued. 'Remember, we used to scream at the Beatles and bark at the Dogs. It was like bloody Battersea Dogs Home, that concert at the Palais in Nottingham, with all the girls yelping, barking and howling. That's right, isn't it, Rox? And we've been barking ever since.' Anne and Rox burst into an uncontrollable fit of laughter. Smudger looked a little nonplussed. Anne slapped him firmly on the thigh.

'Do you remember the party after the gig at the big theatre in Kilburn?'

Smudger looked puzzled. '"That's just the way we were… "'

A thought suddenly came into Roxanne's mind and she spoke for the first time. 'Whatever happened to that dancer, Arry, you were shagging on the tour?'

Smudger coughed and spluttered. 'Erm, she's, erm, Streaky's wife now. So, er, er, how many years since you saw us, Anne?' he stuttered, changing the subject quickly.

'Well, it's forty-one years since I slept with you in that flea-ridden hotel in Brighton.'

'I'll take your word for it.'

Anne grinned. 'We've been reading about you in *The Comet*. By all accounts your prize specimen hasn't shrunk over the years.'

Smudger looked at his watch. 'Now, girls, I need to shake off the trail dust, get some zeds in and lay across my big king-size pine bed.'

Anne looked a little put out. 'Before you go, give us a kiss for old times' sake, before you drift off to dreamland.' She virtually leapt on top of Smudger, her skirt riding up to expose cellulite-studded thighs. In the ensuing tussle Smudger accidentally placed his hands on her right breast. From across the bar Darren Spivey's camera flashed again, again and again.

The next morning the later editions of *The Comet* carried a full-page photo of Smudger's grope with a groupie. The headline ran predictably, 'Old Dog and Bitch on heat – Smudger at it again'.

Smudger was sitting having a late breakfast with Streaky at the Rex Hotel. Streaky glanced at the latest photo calamity and threw the paper to one side. 'This sort of stuff is great for my standing in the local community. One moment you're shagging those stupid teenage tarts, next night you bed some old boiler. Don't you have any sense of morals or decorum in your life? It may be good publicity but it's making us look like a bunch of prats.'

Smudger was taken aback and felt aggrieved. 'Look, I partied in the same room as those chicks and we had a few glasses of wine, but we didn't even take our clothes off. Well, I dropped my trousers once, but that's another matter. I did not have a sexual relationship with those girls.'

'You sound like Bill Clinton.'

'No. Seriously, I got stitched up by that photographer and Fiona with the jumbo jugs. Nothing happened, nothing at all.'

'But what about that old boot last night? You've got one hand on her breast and one on her thigh.'

'Yeah, I know it looked like that in the photo, but that's not how it was. I went to bed last night on my own. "I'm an innocent man".'

Streaky shook his head slowly from side to side. 'You know, I'm all-in after one of these concerts. About all I can do is drink a glass of wine, have a hot shower and go to bed. The only thing I do try to do, if I get time, is have a good massage. That really relaxes me and helps me wind down – you should try it.'

'Yeah, I remember this masseuse in Tahiti – it was amazing. The things she could do.'

Streaky was getting impatient. 'No, I mean a sporting massage – one to relax you, not excite you, to calm you down. I often have one after a round of golf.'

'Yeah, well, each to his own, Streaky.'

'Anyway, we've got those three big nights coming up at Wembley and we're in a five star hotel, complete with every facility. You want to learn to keep it in your trousers, Smudger. Do something like go for a gentle swim or a massage after the gig – that's what I'll be doing.'

Chapter Seventeen

The first night at Wembley was the Dogs' best performance so far. The band was now fully rehearsed and comfortable with each other's musical ability. Every newspaper review had been highly complimentary. The band's album was set to stay at number one in Britain and America for many weeks, and the Dogs' tour had developed into the biggest media and showbiz circus ever seen in Britain. What had started as a fascination for an ageing rock band had progressed into a universal appreciation of the Dogs' unique style – a throwback to the sixties spiced up by contemporary sounds.

After being berated by Streaky for his behaviour, Smudger spent the night after the latest gig reading a book and enjoying a quiet pot of tea before going to bed. Streaky, too, went to his room early and ordered a steak sandwich and a massage. He'd barely taken a bite of the sandwich when there was a knock on the door.

'Hi, I'm Brit Jorgenssen. You ordered a massage?'

'Oh yes. Relief after the strains of the day.'

The Danish masseuse suddenly recognised Streaky. 'Of course. I saw you last night. You play the piano with the Dogs. It was excellent.'

Streaky mumbled out a courteous 'Thank you'.

'You're the most famous person I've had to lay hands on.'

'Really? I hardly think of myself as famous. It's all happened so suddenly.'

Brit started kneading Streaky's shoulders as he lay on his front. 'You are very knotted here and a little tense, but I think we can make you feel a whole lot better and enjoy a good night's sleep. You really are a fit man, Mr Bacon.'

'Well, I play a lot of golf and try to work out a bit at the gym at my golf club. I'm the captain there, you know.'

'Oh, I used to play a little bit of golf back in Copenhagen, but

I don't get much chance here. I'm like a travelling masseuse, helping business people and celebrities in particular. I carry out a lot of work for clients at this hotel.'

'Mmm, yes, that really feels great. I think I'm starting to loosen up a little. You're right; I was perhaps a bit tensed up.'

'No wonder, performing to so many thousand people a night, Mr Bacon.'

'No, no, call me Streaky. Everyone else does.'

'Ahh yes, I see. In my country bacon is very big, so I understand Streaky Bacon. We have the very best smoked bacon near where I come from. It's gorgeous with fresh eggs.'

Brit finished the massage and Streaky paid for her services in cash.

'I can come back tomorrow night and give you some more treatment after your next show, or gig I think you call it.'

'Yes, that's right. That would be very nice. I feel a lot better.'

It was only as she left the room that Streaky noticed her lithe body, pretty face, blonde hair and china blue eyes. At first he'd been oblivious to her looks.

'Right then, see you tomorrow at about eleven o'clock?'

After the Dogs' third sell-out concert at Wembley, Fiona Clamp, who'd been sniffing every scent of the band like a hyperactive bloodhound, was in a huddle in the hotel foyer with snapper, Darren Spivey.

'Daz, this may be something or nothing, but while we've been keeping a close watch on Smudger's shenanigans, I'm not so sure that the straight-laced Streaky isn't going off the rails.'

'How do you make that out, Fi?'

'Well, I've spied this Nordic blonde masseuse emerging from Streaky's room late at night. It just so happens that Streaky's in the honeymoon suite. If you'd seen his stuck-up snobby missus then you couldn't begrudge him a bit of rumpy-pumpy.'

'So, let's get this straight, Fi. You reckon that Streaky's rogering this Scandinavian bit on the side? Now that *would* be some new Dog dirt – after all, we've snapped Smudger with just about everything female that's got a pulse.'

'Tell you what then, Daz, we'll make a few enquiries and see what we can find out. I'll ring the hotel reception.'

Fiona Clamp teetered outside on her stilt-like heels and made a call on her mobile. She snapped the phone shut and walked back to join Darren in the hotel lobby.

'Right, I've just spoken to the receptionist, pretending I'm an agency sorting out personal trainers and massage services, and found out that a certain Danish girl called Brit Jorgenssen will be visiting Streaky for the third night running. Why do I think that's not just for a massage?'

'No way, Fi. The grey-haired old git's having a bit of hanky-panky. Good luck to him. And hopefully good luck for us.'

It was eleven o'clock, and not only was Brian 'Streaky' Bacon looking forward to a massage, he was beginning to enjoy the company of Brit Jorgenssen, as well as her sensual hands moving across his body. He also enjoyed her fits of giggles and sense of fun. He'd started to secretly hope for more than a massage but was rather too shy to ask. He was also guilt-ridden with the thought that if anything pleasurable happened, Arabella might find out. That night he didn't need to be too forward, because Brit made it quite clear that she supplied discreet extra services to celebrities, at a price – and it was a price Streaky was prepared to pay. He'd felt a stirring in his loins the night before, and had lain awake all night wondering if he could entice the nubile Ms Jorgenssen into the king-size bed in the honeymoon suite. If only he'd known that the masseuse, despite his unassuming presence, was star-struck. Streaky nervously fumbled in his wallet to produce a wedge of crisp notes. Brit's blue eyes sparkled.

'That'll do nicely, sir; I don't take credit cards,' she said, and dropped her loosely fitting white uniform to the floor, displaying a vivid blue tattoo of a Viking in a horned helmet above her right breast. She pointed and said, 'We like horny men in Denmark'.

Brit took the initiative and got astride Streaky's sinuous body. Streaky lay there for a while, trying to think of Bach sonatas and Beethoven concertos, before letting out a huge groan and yelling 'I'm coming'. His voice fairly echoed down the corridor, to where a convulsed Darren Spivey spluttered out to a sniggering Fiona Clamp, 'Well, they're not playing Monopoly, that's for sure. If I'm not mistaken, Fi, it's definitely a bit of hanky-panky.'

'Yeah, and quite a short game as well, Daz.'

A quarter of an hour later Streaky, dressed only with a white towel around his waist, kissed Brit passionately as she left the honeymoon suite. The cameras flashed. Darren and Fiona gave a quick high-five and shot off to the nearest lift. 'This Dogs' story's got legs, Fi.'

'Yeah, and plenty of tails, too! Maybe we'll catch Biffo in a sauna with a supermodel.'

'Yeah, I wish. He'd probably still be wearing his grubby vest and pants.'

The next day's *Comet* headline read 'Streaky brings home the Danish bacon'. This time Smudger, Poddy and Biffo couldn't believe what they were seeing on the front page of Britain's sleaziest paper. Streaky had a white-knuckle grasp on his mobile and knew he was about to field the most difficult call of his life. The three other Dogs pretended to be engaged in conversation but could hear Streaky's pleas and defence, with Arabella acting for the prosecution on the other end of the line.

'No, of course I didn't… I had a towel round me because I'd just had a shower… I just gave her a quick peck on the cheek to say thanks… No, thanks for the sports massage… Don't worry, I'm going to sue… The papers have tried to stitch me up… No, there's no need to cut anybody's testicles off… No, I'm not becoming like that sex-crazed chimp, Smudger… You must believe me… Look, why don't you go back to your soft furnishings catalogue, darling… Darling?'

Chapter Eighteen

That afternoon the Dogs were conducting a sound check and short rehearsal for the penultimate show at Wembley. Even Biffo made an involuntary snigger as Streaky's phone went off yet again. The band and crew stopped what they were doing to listen in to Streaky's latest mobile interrogation from Arabella, who, as Poddy remarked, was 'as persistent as an irate wasp'.

'Look, I don't care if Brigadier Aubrey-Awston, Dot and Maurice, the Reverend Norbert, the man with the wig in the paper shop, God, Elvis or the Prime Minister has read about it. It's all lies. I did not have sex with that woman. No, I don't sound like Bill Clinton. I didn't mean to say that… No, not that I didn't have sex with her, no, no, no. What I meant was I didn't want to sound like Bill Clinton… No, I haven't been influenced by "bonk brain" as you so nicely call him; he was in bed by nine thirty. No, on his own, Arabella… No, Smudger is *not* the mastermind behind any kind of fanatical sexual orgy. Well, obviously he may have been like that in the past but not this time. No, I don't mean this was a fanatical sexual orgy and Smudger wasn't there; all I did was have an innocent sports massage after the concert, just the same as I do with Wilma at the golf club after a round – No, I haven't shagged Wilma as well as the Scandinavian slapper. No, no, I didn't mean that; she's not a slapper or a slag but a very respectable girl.'

It was almost as interesting watching as listening. Streaky's facial contortions were matched by his physical gymnastics. He flung his arms to the sky and pretended to beat his head against a wall, before crouching into a near-foetal position with a pained look on his face. This was almost as entertaining as a Dogs' concert. The watching crowd was hooked.

'Arry, nothing happened, OK… I wouldn't know what her body looked like. She kept her tunic on…' At last Streaky gave up. 'Look, I've really got to go.' He pressed the off button and turned to see a dozen people unfreeze and try frantically to look busy. He rolled his eyes heavenwards, turned on his heel and walked out.

Later that afternoon everyone was sitting around relaxed and happy, even Streaky. The Dogs were on the up, there was the tour of the States to come and the money was rolling in. The reviews had been remarkably good, with record sales surging, the publicity machine in overdrive and the Dogs' popularity in America revved up by fascination and fanaticism. The States was on red alert for a tour by the geriatric superstars of rock.

Smudger sidled up to Oops and squeezed her hand. 'C'mon, babe, let's go and have a coffee together.'

'That would be nice, Smudger.'

'What do you want, huh?'

'What, in life or to drink? Let me think, a small cappuccino with cinnamon.'

Smudger smiled. 'Oh yeah, you really are a "cinnamon girl".'

'I don't know that one, Smudger. Was it Dylan?'

'Neal Young, babe.'

As they walked into the coffee lounge, Smudger was still singing, '"Cinnamon girl… " I could be absolutely delirious the rest of my days with you, Oops.'

'I expect you've said that to a few thousand women across the United States.'

Smudger ignored that and signalled to a woman behind the coffee counter. '"Ground Control to Major Tom, commencing countdown engines on", small decaf and small cappuccino with cinnamon.'

Smudger turned towards Oops. 'There's just one problem: have you got any cash?'

'So you offer me a coffee and I've got to pay for it?'

'Oops, I'd buy you all the coffee in Colombia if I could.'

'You've probably bought a little too much from Colombia in your time, and I don't mean coffee. Probably kept the country's economy going for a while.'

'Seems like I've been accused of most things in the papers over the last few months, and I am addicted, but only to you.'

'But you're at least twenty-five years older than me.' She could see he was hurt by that so she added, 'And who wants to go out with a man who can't even buy his girl a coffee?'

'Hey, you're my girlfriend now, are you? Anyway, you're thirty-nine going on twenty-five, and I'm fifty-five going on eighteen, so you've got yourself a toy boy.'

'A toy boy of sixty-five, not fifty-five, I believe. I've done a bit of research and you are sixty-five next month. Poddy is already sixty-five, Streaky has passed sixty-two and Biffo is actually sixty-eight, but could pass for one hundred and eight.'

'You've been checking up on us, Oops.'

'Enjoy your bus pass in a few weeks.'

'But I'm Britain's oldest teenager, babe. That's a fact.'

'So you'll have your birthday during the American tour. There are six venues in a week. The Giants' Stadium in New York, the Detroit Silverdome, Chicago, Frisco, Phoenix and finally the Hollywood Bowl for the last gig. You'll all have heart attacks; I must check our insurance liability.'

Smudger didn't know if she was joking or not, so he took refuge in his usual way. 'You know how they describe me, babe: "born to run"!'

Oops found Smudger's lyrical interludes sometimes charming and sometimes amusing. But lately she found that his past life was irritating her more and more.

'How many of those places in the States are you familiar with?'

'All of them. Spent most of my life travelling backwards and forwards across America. Did a big open-air gig with Airplane in the Big Apple, starred with Santana in San Francisco, jammed and gigged with loads of bands in LA; there was Chicago in Boston and Boston in Chicago—' He caught Oops' look of disbelief. 'That's true. They were all great cats. I did all these blues sessions on bass in Detroit with Muddy, Buddy, Duddy and Sonny. There was Junior, Jimmy, Jonny, Jesse, Blind Willie, Boogie Sam, Freight-train Joe, Cotton Pickin' Petey and Bottleneck Bill. I did this big stadium gig in Frisco with Stevie Ray on guitar, Ginger on drums and me on bass.'

Oops smiled warmly. 'I do believe you, but I sometimes want to believe you make it all up.'

'Well, the papers have made up plenty about me. At least two of those stories about women I've been linked with were not true, but it sure sells records.'

Oops fell quiet for a while, then said, 'Do you realise you'd be seventy-five when I'm forty-nine?'

'So you think we'll be together in ten years – that's cool. Hey, I got you, babe.' He put his arm round her waist. Oops coloured slightly and sucked in the froth and cinnamon on her cappuccino.

The British tour was coming to an end, although Streaky's trial by Arry was not. He'd run up a massive mobile phone bill to try to explain that his fling with the Danish masseuse was a piece of tatty tabloid fiction. Arabella had become prickly and precious, but news of another huge injection of cash into their bank account from Jet Records had done more to calm turbulent waters than any impassioned apologies from Streaky.

As far as the others in the band were concerned, Biffo had soldiered on, combating the pain of piles and the rigours of gout with the help of the good doctor, Chris Stone. He and Streaky were becoming increasingly curmudgeonly and were kept away from press conferences. Poddy had been revelling in his role as front man for the band, but even he was starting to feel very tired. Smudger was still going strong and was anxious to publicise his new active, organic and practically celibate life.

The penultimate show at Wembley was an ecstatic success. At ten o'clock the next morning Poddy and Smudger faced a press conference, then joined Biffo and Streaky, God and Oops for a private meeting. There was plenty of good news for the faded four. They met over coffee and crisp bacon butties in a small conference room and ruminated about the tour. Duke Deckster and Buddy Peabody joined the party. Britain's top DJ was in a hyperactive mood, alternating between his 'street' alter ego and the public-school toff Gilbert Winstanley.

'I made you doggone, doggy dog boys, the coolest curs, baddest old boys and maddest mutts. The pensioner hounds with lots of pounds – I say, this bacon reminds me of brekkers at Eton. We used to have this lumpy porridge like wallpaper paste and then bacon sarnies oozing with butter and fat. Hhmm, scrummy.'

Biffo snorted. 'When I were a lad if we had a fookin' breakfast at all it were a stale fookin' crust. If we were lucky and my old man worked an extra shift at the factory, we got a smear of fookin' dripping.'

Smudger looked thoughtful. 'Yeah, didn't your pa work in that artificial rubber factory?'

Biffo looked even more irritated. 'I know what you're about to say. Yes, it was synthetic rubber and they made condoms. Pity you didn't use more of them and then you wouldn't have fookin' fathered illegitimate kids all over America.'

Poddy was laughing out aloud. 'Biffo's dad was nicknamed Johnnie.'

Biffo lightened up slightly. 'Aye, fookin' thanks for mentioning that.'

Poddy gave Biffo a friendly hug. 'Any which way, enough of all our yesterdays, old fella. When you were young they still had the cowing Black Death.'

Smudger was only half listening. 'Yes, I remember; they were a really spooky heavy three-piece from San Jose. I helped them out with a few gigs at the Filmore.'

Biffo testily interrupted, 'No, we were talking about the Plague.'

Smudger mused for a while. 'Yes, I remember those cats too. The Plague: that was Matty Delport on drums, Jimmy Chang on bass, Simmo Sims on guitar and Fez Farrell on keyboards. They were from Santa Barbara way.'

Oops put down her coffee. 'I don't think this chat's quite in sync.'

Godfrey chortled, 'Well, lads, do you want to hear the good news or the good news?'

Poddy gulped down a huge mouthful. 'Well, tell you what: we'll take the good news first, any which way.'

Godfrey's grin broadened. 'Well, actually Duke has all the details. Our people in the States have done a stonking publicity job. You're on fire and nothing can put out the flames.'

Duke Deckster slid on his scholarly spectacles. 'Yes, chaps, your sales have not just beaten, but battered, the opposition. You are one, two, three, four and five in the charts. The album is number one and the sales figures are off the scale.'

Godfrey nodded in agreement. 'I think some of you know that the US tour is now a six-date sell-out at just about the biggest venues across the country, ending at the Hollywood Bowl. You'll be supported by a new hip-hop star called Jerk Snapper. We've got to dot the *i*'s and cross the *t*'s with you guys and Buddy on a new deal. We'll try to get that signed in the next few days. It's for the American tour, a new British and European tour, a live album and another new studio album. I think you'll find all the details to your liking.'

Buddy thumbed through a wedge of documents and prodded a few keys on his laptop. 'I've been talking to God and Oops over the last few days. There're only a few tiny bits and pieces to be sorted out, then we'll talk it through and sign it, if it's OK with you fellas.'

Poddy put his hand on Biffo's shoulder. 'Good, we'll be able to buy you a truckload of vests and pants.'

Streaky looked worried. 'What's the plan after all this? After all, we're not getting any younger, and we'll be away from home for ages.'

Poddy interrupted. 'Well, Biffo can't get any cowing older.'

Buddy held up his hands to regain attention.

'Guys, the broad plan is we sign the new contract for the tours and albums, then there's a break next summer. We'll sort out what we do in the future after that.'

Streaky didn't look convinced. After years of tight control of money and his life, he was beginning to fear he was losing control of it all. The episode with the masseuse had rattled him. This wasn't the way a bank manager should behave.

After ironing out a few details, Poddy and Biffo left for a game of chess. Godfrey moved on to another meeting with Duke, while Streaky departed to make yet another placatory phone call to Arabella.

'So it's just you and me left, Oops,' Smudger observed.

'You've still got your tracksuit on with a towel around your neck.'

'That's right, babe. In the gym at seven for a commando-style workout before a healthy breakfast.'

'But you've just gobbled a bacon buttie.'

'I only like the lean bits; that's why I like you. Don't like fat, and there's not an ounce on your body, babe.'

Oops switched the conversation back to him.

'I have to admit you are in amazing shape after the alleged life you've led, although I take it all with a large spoonful of salt.'

'"You are the sunshine of my life".'

'"You make me feel like a natural woman". How about that one, Smudger?'

'Pretty good, you're getting on my wavelength.'

In the corner of the hotel, Poddy was enjoying a reunion with Big Eric and Little Jimmy. They had joined a lavish corporate outing for the final concert. The terminator, exterminator and inseminator had a lot of gossip to catch up on. A pot of tea replaced the usual pints but the conversation needed little stimulation. Big Eric couldn't wait to give Poddy an update.

'Derby have signed this big ugly git from Rochdale up front. He's got everything apart from any fucking talent. That Gordon – you know, Gormless Gordon – has walked out on his missus and made off with that floozie who works in Crocker's Chemists. And you'll never believe this one – that police inspector Norman Whatsisface is having a sex-change operation.'

Poddy guffawed. 'Suppose he'll be losing his truncheon.'

Jimmy piped in, 'Aye, never thought he had the balls for the job. By the way, it all seems to have gone a bit quiet on the Smudger front. Nothing in the papers lately. What's going on?'

Poddy poured a cup of tea. 'It's true he's usually at it like a frog up a pump, but he's been like a bloody sedated monk for the last couple of weeks. In bed early, on his own, works out in the cowing gym and eats rabbit food.'

Big Eric leaned back in his chair, looking puzzled. 'Maybe he's suffering from sexual exhaustion after all these years. Perhaps the novelty's worn off. It did with my missus after a few months. That's when I turned to Marston's Pedigree. Beer never talks back.'

'That stuff does,' said Jimmy and let out a loud fart. 'As for Smudger, you know what they say: once a randy git always a randy git, even if you're an old one. Smudger was the only third-former with gonorrhoea. Most of us thought it was some sort of exotic cheese at the time.'

Eric chuckled. 'At that age we thought that syphilis was the name of our great aunt.'

Poddy nodded vigorously in agreement. 'And when that chlamydia appeared we all thought it was some type of cowing plant.'

All three were laughing heartily as Poddy burst into a raucous song. 'Some die of drinking whisky and some of drinking beer, some die of diabetes and some of diarrhoea, but of all the world's diseases there's none that can compare to the drip, drip, drip on the end of your prick of the British gonorrhoea.'

Jimmy pointed at Poddy. 'Don't think you'll be opening the US tour with that one.'

'Perhaps not. Any which way, lads, have you heard this one? Bloke walking down the street. Sees this gorgeous girl. She smiles at him. So he looks back at her a little quizzically. He thinks he knows her. She smiles again and says "Don't you remember me? You're the father of one of my children". So the guy feels a bit guilty and panicked, and thinks for a while and says "I'm sorry, were you the girl in that club the other night I gave one from behind on the pool table while you gave my mate a blowjob?" And she says "No, I'm your son's English teacher".'

Poddy, Big Eric and Little Jimmy brayed with laughter in unison and quaffed their cups of tea as though they were imaginary pint pots of best bitter.

It was supposed to be a relaxed build-up to the climax of the sell-out tour, with no drama and lots of celebration before the final gig at Wembley. Poddy sat in a small reception room playing chess with Biffo.

'I think that's a crafty little move, old chap, and talking of crafty moves I see that Smudger is now claiming that he's celibate.'

'More like a fookin' halibut. Fishy, slimy and full of crap.' Biffo winced in pain as he moved his queen. 'Fookin' 'ellfire, I'm in bloody agony.'

'Where? Is it your Farmer Giles or your pig's snout?'

'It's been getting worse over the last few days. It really hurts when I play.' He held his right arm.

'Well, I'm not a top physician, but I don't think you can get piles or gout there,' said Poddy.

'It's fookin' painful, whatever it is.'

Poddy decided to find Dr Stone. The doctor grabbed his bag and hurried to the scene. 'OK, Biffo let's take a look. Where does it hurt?'

'In my fookin' armpit.'

Poddy grimaced. 'Rather you than me, doc. First his arse, then his feet, now his cowing armpit.'

Biffo unbuttoned his shirt and lifted up his arm. Poddy turned away as the doctor made a close examination.

'Well, it's pretty nasty, but nothing much to worry about. You've got a large boil developing. I'll need to lance it, then dress it and apply something to alleviate the soreness when you're hitting those drums.'

Poddy was already heading for the door.

The doc gave Biffo an injection for his gout, a pain-killing spray for his piles and some cream to stop his boil causing too much discomfort. It looked as though the show could go on.

It did, with a phenomenal reception for the band. But the after-show party was subdued. The touring had been hard work and the old boy band was starting to feel like the old blokes band that they really were. Biffo was even more angry and aggravated than usual, and the novelty of the new-found fame was wearing thin for Poddy, who was starting to feel distinctly homesick and increasingly weary. Streaky was becoming more distant and detached, while Smudger had become reclusive apart from his chats with Oops. Here, at the height of their success, the Dogs' commitment to fame and fortune was starting to stray.

In his untidy office Dick Rodger adjusted his brown, one hundred percent polyester tie, and stirred three sachets of sugar into a coffee. He sat on his desk, drawing on a cigarette and sucking the rim of the polystyrene cup while forensically examining the first edition of a new Comet Group publication called *Scandies in Scanties*. Fiona Clamp exploded through the door. Dick Rodger threw down the magazine and spread the morning edition of *The Comet* across his desk. The headline read, 'SEX DOG SMUDGER GIVES UP HIS BITCHES'.

'That's a bit hard to believe, Fi, and not very good for sales. More likely he's saving all his efforts for the American tour.'

Fiona Clamp poured herself a cup of coffee. 'Maybe. Is everything sorted out for me to report on the Dogs in the States?'

'Yes, but their people are starting to make life very difficult. They're travelling everywhere by private chartered jet and will be cocooned away from press and public with a complete hotel floor to themselves.'

'I know who's behind that. It's that self-important, overgrown schoolgirl Olivia Ponsonby-Smart.' Fi was annoyed that Oops was keeping her away from the Dogs. 'She thinks she's running the whole show. I think she's trying to take credit for everything.'

'Well get over there and keep this Dogs stuff going. And I don't mean the stuff about Smudger giving up sex, drugs and rock'n'roll. Circulation figures are fantastic, the share price in the Comet Group is up and there's a record Christmas bonus on the way, but only because we're coming up with insider stories. You must have spoken to our guy in New York, Jerry Ziebahrt. You'll get a lot of help from him; he's red-hot when it comes to showbiz contacts.'

'When do I leave?'

'Tomorrow morning. We've booked you into the same hotel the Dogs are staying in, but you'll have to infiltrate the party in your own inimitable way.' He smiled, looking somewhere in the region of her chest. Fiona Clamp seemed to use her protruding breasts as a kind of navigational and directional aid. She pointed them towards the door and strode out.

A fragment of polystyrene was stuck to Dick Rodger's lip, and a few drips of sticky, sugary coffee seeped onto the grubby collar of his white shirt. *The Comet* editor picked up *Scandies in Scanties* again, along with that month's *Horny Babes*, to read while he finished his coffee.

An air traffic controllers' dispute held up the Dogs' flight to New York, making them tired and irritable. They arrived at JFK airport at one in the morning to be greeted by a massive crowd as they walked out of the airport to a waiting limousine. They were pelted with rubber Zimmer frames, incontinence pants and vests. Biffo scowled, but a look from Oops saw him rearrange his face into a fixed grin. Oops could tell things were not right. This wasn't going to be an easy tour. Thank god it was a short one.

Chapter Nineteen

The Comet's campaign had caught on in America. 'Pensioner Power' had crossed the Atlantic with the impact of a tidal wave. The Dogs had been delivered to add a volume to Uncle Sam's social history. The Beatles caused some tremors in the States; the Dogs were off the Richter scale. Newspapers and magazines were filled with special supplements and features on the Dogs; TV news stations presented live programmes on the arrival of the geriatric quartet. This was to be a strictly regimented tour. All the Dogs were scheduled to see were the insides of hotel rooms, limousines, planes, dressing rooms and concert venues. Oops had planned everything meticulously. The old boy band were contracted to do a short press conference after every show, and appear once on television on a coast-to-coast network chat show with the number one chat man, Hank Zacharias. By the time they were billeted in their hotel overlooking Central Park it was two thirty in the morning. They were dog-tired.

The Dogs had travelled with a large entourage of technicians and experts in staging a big show. It was like an army on the march, with the generals being Godfrey Vanderbloom, Olivia Ponsonby-Smart and Buddy Peabody. The first day was to be hectic, with a get-together in the morning, sound check and rehearsal in the afternoon and then the first big show at the Giants' stadium. A meeting was scheduled for eleven o'clock that morning to familiarise the band with the schedule once again, underline the strict press and media policy, and run through the order of songs for the concerts.

Oops was already working through piles of paper and hammering out more details of the programme on a laptop when, promptly at eleven, Smudger joined her, dressed in his customary tracksuit with a towel around his neck.

'Fifteen minutes on the rowing machine, fifteen minutes cycling like Lance Armstrong, fifteen minutes burning up the treadmill and fifteen minutes pumping iron.'

'You must be the fittest cat in the pension queue.'

Smudger continued to ignore any references to his age or any signs that Oops might not be one hundred percent into him.

'Just you and me, Oops, together in the Big Apple. I could show you around town, take you to Bloomingdale's and Saks on Fifth Avenue. We could go to Greenwich Village where I used to play in the same clubs as Bobby – Bobby Dylan – and Youngy – Neal Young – and Jimi. I could take you to a little Italian place in Tribeca where they do the best pasta in the city. I'd just love to wine and dine you.'

'Hmm, talking of whine, w-h-i-n-e, Biffo is getting really irritable. He's just about impossible. I can't believe it; he's made a few million in a matter of weeks and acts as though he's going through a sadistic torture process.'

'Yeah, me and Biffo aren't getting on too well.'

'I don't think you ever did.'

'Well, he used to dislike me, then he became quite hostile towards me, now he actively hates me.'

'Well, even Poddy's finding it hard to stay in his good books.'

'Yeah, after his piles and gout, and now that horrible boil under his armpit, it's all added to his aura.'

'If you don't mind, I've not had any breakfast yet. The thought of Biffo's armpit would put anybody off eating for weeks.'

Smudger changed the subject. 'You know, I was serious, babe, about a night out on the town.' Oops didn't look at him.

'You know how tightly organised we are. Everything has got to be spot on for the first concert. The critics here will eat us alive if we foul up the first show.'

'Babe, we're so well-rehearsed we could play those songs in our sleep. Got to be living for the city. I once did an impromptu jam session in a basement club off Broadway with Frank Zappa and John Lennon on guitars, Keith Moon on drums, me on bass.'

At that moment the hollow-eyed, skeletal figure of Biffo drifted into the room, looking like an agitated zombie.

'Talking all that fookin' gob shite again. Everyone you claim to have played with are all long gone. I fookin' would be if I could get out of this hellhole. The Big Apple, more like the fookin' rotten apple. A whole week of this fookin' purgatory.'

Oops looked up, peering above her glasses. 'Good morning, Biffo, I trust you slept well.'

'As a matter of fact, no, I fookin' didn't. My fookin' gout was agony after that bastard flight and I would've slept better in a hammock across the central reservation of the M1.'

Smudger tried to pacify Biffo. 'Look, c'mon mate, if you ask me—'

'I'm not your fookin' mate, never have been and why the fookin' 'ell would I want to ask you about anything.'

Biffo started to make a cup of tea with a bag on a string. 'Could do with some proper tea with some flavour, made in a pot. This stuff tastes like fookin' piss.'

He sat down at the end of the table as far away from Oops and Smudger as he could possibly be, turned his back and stared at the wall.

Oops just sighed and continued working through some last-minute alterations to the schedule. She didn't have time to be a nanny at the moment. Smudger flipped through the suggested song schedule for the concerts, which were to end with an encore of an extended version of 'Treat Me like a Dog'.

Godfrey and Buddy were next into the room, both apologising for being a quarter of an hour late. It was another fifteen minutes before a rather flustered Streaky appeared. As he stumbled out an apology his mobile rang. Oops was getting impatient. 'Look, Streaky, can you deal with that later?'

Streaky, usually shy and docile, snapped in anger, 'No, this is important!' He walked out of the room but left the door slightly ajar so the conversation, or rather monologue, seeped into the room.

'No, I had no one in my room last night… Smudger didn't get some old friends together for an orgy… No, this is not a glorified tour of massage parlours… For god's sake, Arabella, can't you let it rest… No, that Danish woman hasn't followed me over here… We'll do the concerts then stay in our rooms… No, we'll be going to bed early on our own… And no, that sex-crazed chimp Smudger isn't influencing me. Look, why don't you stick to the gossip at the ladies' luncheon club!'

Streaky sneaked back in, not realising his phone call had been overheard by everyone. Smudger tipped back the rim of his brown suede cowboy hat. 'So, sex-crazed chimp. That's not very cool, man.'

'You shouldn't be listening to private conversations.'

'Come on, we couldn't help it.'

'Thanks to you my whole marriage is under strain.'

'What's it to do with me if you take a fancy to a Danish pastry.'

'I did not have sex with that woman.'

'Hey now, wasn't that Bill Clinton? Well, *The Comet* think you did have sex with that woman.'

'Well, fuck *The Comet!*'

Godfrey stood up and tried to restore calm. 'Look, guys, easy. Our arrival here has gone down a storm. I know that was an awful journey and everyone is a little irritated, but let's just stay calm and concentrate on the day ahead. We've got a mini rehearsal and sound check this afternoon.'

Poddy was the last to arrive. He looked tired and dishevelled, with dark rings around his eyes. 'Sorry, I sort of cowing well overslept. I had a nightmare about Biffo's boil exploding and drowning me.'

For once Biffo took offence at one of Poddy's jibes. 'Ha bleeding ha. If you had a problem like that you'd have been screaming in pain, you big fookin' Jessie.'

'Hey, easy, old fella.'

'Fook off!'

Godfrey stood up again and held his arms up above his head. 'Come on now, this is getting daft. We're arguing like squabbling kids in a nursery. Let's work together.'

Smudger tactlessly burst into song. 'C'mon, guys, "let's work together". Hey, remember Bob "The Bear" Hite? We did a double act in this club—'

Biffo threw down his teacup and smashed the saucer. 'Yeah, he's another one who's fookin' died after working with you. No one else is left alive. It's just a fookin' pity you still are.'

At that moment Oops yelled at the top of her voice, 'All of you, just SHUT UP.'

Everyone looked, except for Smudger, who settled back in his chair and smiled. 'Sorry, babe.'

The prickliness started affecting everything. The band seemed to have lost their sense of balance as well as their sense of proportion. Poddy caught his forehead on the door of the limousine. A large jagged gash bled profusely. He held a handkerchief over the wound. In the stadium dressing room, Dr Chris Stone inserted nine stitches to close up the cut. He also administered a mild tranquiliser to Streaky, who was both agitated and exhausted from his phone calls. Then he had to tend to Biffo's various ailments and patch him up to play the drums for another gig. The result was that out of adversity the concert was a triumph. New York had virtually adopted the Dogs, and their performance that night was extraordinary. Biffo was manic on drums, Streaky gave a virtuoso performance, Smudger was calm and Poddy expended enough energy to light up the whole of Manhattan. They performed no less than four encores, including a ten-minute version of 'Treat Me like a Dog'. For half an hour afterwards the audience remained behind, cheering and chanting:

> *You treat me like a dog*
> *You treat me like a dog*
> *You've got me yelping and a yapping, snarling and a snapping*
> *Cos you treat me like a dog*

At the finish, the stage was almost knee-deep in the paper incontinence pants, inflatable Zimmer frames, vests, vitamins and rubber walking sticks that had been dished out by the American newspapers. Even the press conference afterwards was lively, as Poddy and Smudger charmed the gathering with their wit and repartée. The evening's triumph was reflected by celebratory articles in the papers next day. The *New York Times* devoted its complete front page and a huge pullout to the Dogs.

Fiona Clamp rang the bell at *The Comet*'s bureau on the twentieth floor of a block near the Rockefeller Centre. A tall, skinny man with thick, rimless glasses and a shock of grey, frizzy hair met her in the reception.

'Hi, we've talked so often over the phone. I'm Jerry Ziebahrt. You must be Fiona Twin Peaks... I... I mean Clamp.'

'No, don't worry. I'm aware everyone calls me that. I take it as a compliment really.'

'I'll just call you Fi.'

'They call me that too,' she replied.

Jerry was distracted as the buttons on the front of Fiona's white silk blouse were nearly bursting. They looked like bullets about to be fired.

'So, you've got all those fantastic exclusives on the Dogs. It's been great stuff. Everyone's been reading it over here. In fact, it's by far the biggest soap in the United States.'

Fiona smiled as she realised from the way he was staring at her breasts that Jerry was going to be no problem. As soon as men talked to her tits she had the power. 'You've helped out a lot with the contacts for all those revelations about Smudger's little liaisons over here.'

Jerry held up one finger. 'And I might just have something else.'

'What, more ex-wives, girlfriends, groupies?'

'No, not exactly. Come through to my office.'

Jerry ushered Fiona through to an oak-panelled room with a fine view over Manhattan.

'Now, this may give the Dogs' tale another extraordinary twist. A freelance guy we use who's based in Sacramento sent us this batch of black-and-white photos. He wants a lot of dough for them, and you'll see why.'

Jerry spread six slightly blurred images across the desk. They showed Smudger hugging, cuddling, and in one shot kissing, a fresh-faced lad of about twenty.

Fiona stared silently for a few minutes, examining the pictures one by one.

'Good god, so the world's most sex-crazed crinkly is really bisexual? Incredible. My dad used to play cricket and called them all-rounders.'

Jerry looked amused. 'What does that mean?'

Fiona explained, 'It's a cricket term.'

Jerry frowned.

'You know,' went on Fiona, 'it's like baseball, but with a point to it. He bats and bowls, or you might say "slugs" and "pitches".'

Jerry thought about it. 'Yeah, I think I've got the gist.'

Fiona lit up a cigarette and inhaled deeply. 'We've done so many headlines on Smudger it's been like a separate industry. The file on the Dogs must be the biggest in the system. One moment he's Britain's most sex-mad senior citizen, then he claims to be celibate, and now it's revealed he's bi.'

'Well, maybe he's renounced women in the last few months.'

'No, I can tell you he hasn't from personal – I mean, from personal conversations.'

'I'm sure Dick back in London will like this one.' That was Jerry's cue to stare at her bulging chest as it fought to free itself from the flimsy material of her blouse.

Fiona smiled wolfishly. 'I'm sure he will. These pics are worth a few bucks.'

That morning the Dogs were flown to Detroit for the second gig at the Silverdome. They all sat apart on the plane. Biffo was at the back, reading a new biography on Trotsky. Poddy slumped across two seats, reading the tributes in the papers. Smudger was enjoying a lot of banter and a glass of red wine with Oops, while Streaky sat at the front of the plane, staring vacantly into space. The four members of the band did not exchange a word on the flight. Oops had decided to ignore things for now. The team would only have eight hours to set up the show, so she considered there would be no time for more tantrums.

In the dressing room beforehand, the mood was flat. Even Poddy was uncharacteristically subdued and withdrawn. He was suffering from complete exhaustion and was troubled by Biffo turning against him. He spent most of the afternoon prostrate on a large sofa. Biffo just ignored everyone and everything and read his book. Streaky filled his time by playing his favourite pieces of Rachmaninov and Beethoven on a small upright piano, while Smudger hovered around Oops. At one point Biffo threw his book down and muttered that he was going to get some fresh air. He wandered around and eventually found a passageway out of the vast arena. Blinded by bright sunlight, he was confronted by a microphone, camera and reporter.

'This is Brad Masterston live at the Silverdome and can you

believe it, we've been joined by the Dogs' drummer, Charlie 'Biffo' Bear.'

As Biffo tried to turn and leave, Brad put an arm around his shoulder and pulled him towards the microphone.

'Biffo, how much are the Dogs looking forward to putting on a show in Detroit?'

'We're not.'

Brad Masterson took this to be some kind of dry and peculiarly English wit and laughed, 'No really, I suppose you can't wait for the gig.'

'Can't wait to go home more like.'

Masterston sniggered. 'No seriously, how much are you enjoying your tour to the States?'

'I've told you once – I'm not. It's shite.'

'Shite, that's a new one,' said Brad. 'Is this your first time in Detroit?'

'Detroit? More like detritus!'

'Any message for the good folks of the US of A?'

'Yeah – fook off!'

Biffo walked away, back into the auditorium, leaving a shocked Brad Masterson trying to explain the outburst to his producer.

The short interview had been recorded in *The Comet*'s office in New York. Fiona Clamp was excitedly talking to Dick Rodger on the telephone.

'You'll never believe it – it just gets better and better. We've got a double Dog lead for *The Comet*. Smudger is bisexual, and Biffo tells America to "fook off" – you might need a few asterisks on the front page, Dick. These stories are going to run right across America, but we'll have them in our paper before anybody else.'

Oops, Godfrey and Jet Records' PR and Publicity department reacted quickly to run a fire-fighting operation followed by a major campaign to maintain that Biffo's outburst was just a joke that went a little too far. They also claimed that Biffo didn't realise it was a live broadcast and was just having a bit of fun. Luckily his four-letter-word tirade seemed to cause little offence and passed off with hardly any reaction, mainly because the

American public couldn't understand his accent and in the main had no idea what 'shite' and 'fook' meant. Fortunately, the concert went well. Back in England the full transcript of the interview, plus pictures, were widely published.

Before the third concert date in Chicago, Smudger read *The Comet*'s stories and saw the pictures of himself and the young man under excited headlines. He kept his own counsel, apart from a confidential chat with Oops, but didn't seem at all bothered or perplexed by the revelations. A few hours later at the press conference, after another successful concert, Smudger was pursued with questions on the latest story about his private life.

'Smudger, can you tell us about this relationship?'

'You can make up your own conclusions. After all, you usually do.'

'Who is the young man in the photos?'

'I can't tell you that.'

'What are your feelings about the story?'

'Well, you can make up your own mind; it doesn't bother me.'

'Was this a lover?'

'I love him very much. Look, cats, can we get back to the music?'

Smudger smilingly waved away any further questions about the pictures with the young man.

The rest of the band was by now no longer talking to each other, so they didn't bother him with questions. Relations were not so much strained as tight as a dog's lead with a twelve-stone Rottweiller pulling it. The band had become snarling curs, just waiting to see who would snap and bite first. Biffo only talked to Dr Stone. Streaky's only conversations were strained, on his mobile to Arabella. Poddy was completely wiped out after every night's performance, and Smudger spent practically all his time with Oops. But the performances were still being enthusiastically received. Record sales were increasing, with the Dogs still holding the top five positions in the singles chart and album sales setting a record that was never likely to be equalled.

At the end of the set in San Francisco the Dogs gave their all for a final encore of 'Treat Me like a Dog'. As they finished, Biffo started contorting and gasping as he flailed his arms around the drum kit. The crowd yelled, stamped and cheered in appreciation. Biffo gasped again and looked to be involved in a gurning contest as a tortured close-up of him was displayed on the arena's big screens. He threw down a drumstick and, to more wild applause, fell across the kit, scattering drums, cymbals, pedals and sticks in all directions. At that moment Dr Chris Stone sprinted across the stage, which was plunged into darkness. The crowd whistled, enjoying the theatrical end to the concert. Dr Stone started applying chest massage to Biffo, followed by mouth-to-mouth resuscitation. He administered an injection and called for an ambulance. Staff and paramedics on hand worked very rapidly. Within minutes Biffo had been driven away and taken to a nearby hospital. The audience looking at the darkened stage were unaware of the drama that had unfolded in front of them. Everyone was still on their feet chanting for another encore as medics were getting to work on Biffo Bear in the emergency room at the hospital. The band was smuggled out of the auditorium and the press conference was cancelled.

Back at the hotel the three remaining members of the band gathered together in Poddy's room. They were silent and very subdued. Eventually Dr Stone and Oops joined them. Oops gave a deep sigh. 'Look, I'd better let the doc explain.'

'OK, well, it's in many ways good news. Biffo had a heart attack.'

Before the rest of the band could react, he added, 'Fortunately, the unit at the hospital here is one of the best in the world. He was treated very quickly and there is likely to be little or no lasting damage. With a good rest he'll be completely back to normal. There's technically no such thing as a mild heart attack, but, if there was, this would be very mild. Thankfully he received prompt and excellent treatment.'

A tear ran down Poddy's cheek. 'Poor old sod!'

Dr Stone consoled him. 'Listen, Poddy, he's going to need you. I've noticed you're the only one who's really close to him.'

'Yeah, we grew up a bit together, although he's a lot older than me. He gave me my first old battered guitar and some sort of instruction.' He wiped away another tear and looked at the doctor. 'I've never told anybody before – it's one of those things that we don't really ever talk about – but he's my half brother.'

Chapter Twenty

There were only two gigs to go: one in Phoenix, and the tour finale at the Hollywood Bowl. Biffo's on-stage heart attack had now become the biggest story in the Dogs' tale so far, although he was already out of intensive care and recuperating in a lavish private room in a hospital in San Francisco. Poddy conducted a long press conference and paid tribute to his old mate, but with two concerts left a big decision had to be made. Should the Dogs turn tail or find a way of keeping the show on the road?

A huge press pack was besieging the band's hotel when they arrived in Phoenix. Inside, Godfrey Vanderbloom gathered Poddy, Streaky, Smudger and Oops together.

'The latest bulletin we've had from the hospital is that Biffo can fly home in a week's time, and he shouldn't suffer any lasting problem from the attack.'

Poddy frowned. 'What are we going to do now, though? We'll have to go home, too, because there's no one who can take his place. He's a one-off as a drummer.'

And a one-off in a few other ways too, Godfrey thought, but confined himself to the raising of an eyebrow.

'It's not as bad as you think,' he said. 'I've been in touch with Buzz Diablo.'

Smudger was first to react. 'Buzz Diablo? What, *the* Buzz Diablo? Hang on a minute, is he still alive?'

'Just about,' said Godfrey. 'He's seventy-five, a bit of a veteran even by your standards, but he's already listened to your material and reckons he could step in, no bother.'

'No bother, no cowin' bother?' Poddy's pent-up frustrations exploded. 'If it's that easy why don't you get my great auntie Doris to cowin' well step in and use her knitting needles as drumsticks? Biffo's one of the best in the business, and you think you can drag some bar steward with a daft-sounding name off the street to do the job. Well, fookin' great. Why don't you have a flick through the phone directory to see if you can find someone with an even dafter name to replace me, too, if it's that fookin' easy.'

Smudger could see Godfrey was rattled by the outburst and stepped in. 'Hey, hey, Buddy, easy now. Just stay cool, don't be a fool.' he said soothingly to Poddy. 'This guy Buzz is the best there is – apart from Biffo, of course,' he added quickly, as Poddy glowered at him. 'Look, yeah, he's a bit of a strange cat. He looks like one of those cartoon Mexicans – you know, a bit short, and squat as a bullfrog, with a yard brush moustache and a sombrero the size of Dolly Parton's bra. But he's played with Count Basie and Duke Ellington in the fifties, as well as all the top blues singers.'

Godfrey saw his chance. 'Yes, yes, that's right.' He grabbed some notes and read them out. 'Listen to this. He formed the Buzz Diablo Big Band and the Buzz Diablo Quartet. He also got quite a reputation for staging private concerts for presidents and heads of state all over the world. He's really, really good. We'll find somewhere for a rehearsal and do a full run-through of all the material before the show tonight. It's not fantastic, but it's the best we can do at this short notice. Look, I'm as hacked off as you. I'd like to complete these two gigs and go home.'

It took the sting out of Poddy's argument, and he, Streaky, and Smudger nodded tersely in agreement.

'Anyway, while we're getting shock announcements out of the way, I've got another one,' said God after a pause. 'I'm retiring.'

As the band members took this in, Godfrey went to the door and opened it to let in Oops and Buddy carrying trays of champagne and glasses.

'Even God has to rest sometime,' he said. 'And this is a celebration,' he added, trying to raise spirits. 'I'm not going for good. I'll still be doing some consultancy work.'

Godfrey filled the champagne glasses. Smudger was first to take a sip. 'Best of luck from all the chicks and cats in the business; "now it's time to leave the capsule if you dare".' Everyone raised their glasses as Buddy Peabody proposed a toast to Godfrey Vanderbloom. As they sipped the drink he asked, 'Sorry to be selfish, God, but what's gonna happen in future, especially for us?'

God put down his glass. 'Well, I'll still be watching over you like a guardian angel. I'm still contracted to carry out a little work for Jet. There are a few loose ends to tie up, but in the future you'll be talking to a new MD for Jet Records, Brett Radische.'

Poddy looked a little worried. 'So what's he like?'

'Well, I took him on board. He's a former New York attorney who's specialised in the entertainments business and has worked for us for some time. Brett's a bit of a hotshot, and a hothead at times, but his heart's in the right place and he knows what he's doing. He certainly knows how to make a deal.'

Buddy still looked a little uncertain. 'So who's in charge from this moment on?'

God smiled. 'Well, technically I've handed over the baton to Brett, although I've made the arrangements for the final concerts and sorted out the deal with Buzz Diablo.'

'So what's the plan for these last two gigs?' asked Streaky.

'Well,' God hesitated and took a sidelong glance at Poddy; 'Buzz is confident he can play with only a short rehearsal, but having such a famous name comes at a price. Well, two prices really.'

Poddy chuntered to himself, showing little enthusiasm. 'Aye, and what the cowing hell would they be?'

'Well, first we've had to pay him per performance, and as you can imagine, he's not exactly as cheap as chips. Then we've had to agree to his performing a big drum solo in two of the numbers – but there's a big plus in that idea, as one of them can replace Biffo's recorded rap in 'Treat Me like a Dog'. There's no doubt he'll also embellish things a bit with a few fills and frills. But it should all go well. He's still the best drummer in the business – almost.'

Poddy tried to look bored and uninterested, Streaky was obviously worried and perplexed, and Smudger was himself a little uneasy, the perma-smile not quite so pronounced.

And before they knew it, Buzz Diablo was there in front of them.

'I wonder how tall he is when he stands up,' said Poddy bitterly, as a small, round man strutted into the middle of the rehearsal room. His huge hat almost drowned him, and, when he tilted his head back, all that could be seen was his moustache, twitching like a demented caterpillar.

There was no time for pleasantries; the band got straight down to work. Buzz disappeared behind his hat and drums and did indeed add a few extras, working in some elaborate fills and drum solos. Before long he'd taken charge of the rehearsal. He added quite a bit to Biffo's style, with his whirling arms and pumping legs, his face almost completely obliterated by the monster 'tache and huge hat. At the end of the session Poddy, Smudger and Streaky had the chance for a proper introduction. Streaky nervously shook hands and rather formally added, 'Nice of you to join us, Mr Diablo.'

Buzz cast aside his sombrero to reveal a shock of heavily-dyed raven-black hair. 'Hey, if you gringos had a few weeks working with me I could turn you into real musicians rather than bit part players. I can tell you this pop stuff is pretty simple to play after jazz.'

Smudger muttered under his breath, 'Yeah, rave on, man, you got me reelin.'

Poddy looked furious, but Streaky nodded in agreement. 'I remember you played for President Kennedy and the Clintons.'

'That's not all, boy. I've played for just about every president of the USA in the White House: Eisenhower, Johnson, Nixon, Ford, Carter and Reagan. Why, Lyndon and Ike both had a go on my drum kit. Gave them both a bit of tuition. I can tell you that both Georgie Bush Senior and Junior got my Quartet to play to visiting leaders at Camp David. Now ain't that something, boys! Young Bill Clinton tried playing a bit of sax with my Quartet, wasn't up to much though. You'll never believe this one; at the time I played a series of private parties for Jack Kennedy, I was also flying out to play for Khrushchev at the Kremlin, I'll tell ya! Now ain't that something, too! I've played for Mao in Peking, Castro in Cuba, Mandela in South Africa, Gaddafi in a big tent in Libya, Chirac in France and your very own Tommy Blair in Britain at that Chequered House. Yes, siree, that's Buzz by Presidential appointment.'

While he was talking Buzz Diablo didn't seem to draw breath. You couldn't see his lips move under the monster moustache.

Poddy was looking pained and aggravated as the Mexican drummer man continued, 'I'll tell you, boys, and y'all know, I've worked with all the greats, but they've all worked with me. The Count and the Duke, Woody Herman, Louis Armstrong, Brubeck, Coltrane, Miles Davis, Dizzy Gillespie, Oscar Peterson, Errol Garner, Billie Holiday and Ella. And I'll tell you I sorted out a lot of arrangements for those folks. Hey now, Buzz Diablo: 'have sticks will travel'. Now ain't that the way, boys. Anyway, I'll sit in tonight and tomorrow and give you gringos a bit of polish and a real show. It's a pity I haven't got a little longer. I reckon I could lick you boys into shape.'

He pointed a drum stick at Streaky. 'Hey you, boy, you could be a half decent jazz player with a bit of schooling from Buzz. But I'll see you guys tonight. I always get in a siesta before a concert. Old habits never die. You boys should try it, too.'

Buzz Diablo straightened his big sombrero – he was five feet three with it off and five feet eleven with it on – and swaggered off the stage. He was barely out of earshot as Poddy blasted out, 'What a fucking pompous little arsehole!'

Even Smudger looked slightly irritated. 'All those stories he came out with. I can't stand all that bragging and name-dropping about all the people he's played with. I bet only half of it is true.'

Poddy started to mutter under his breath. 'Coming from you… Oh, forget it.'

Poddy had lost a considerable amount of weight over the last few days of the tour and had last displayed his chirpy personality at the press conference in New York. Dr Chris Stone had rejoined the tour after checking that Biffo was getting the best possible treatment. Poddy summoned him to his hotel room.

'Look doc, I'm just about exhausted. I'm completely knackered. I don't think I can get through one more, let alone two cowing concerts. I just feel shattered, shagged, knackered, buggered, fucked and fucked off… completely fucked and pissed off—'

'OK, I think I've got the picture. You don't exactly sit on the fence. I'll give you a thorough check-over. I must confess you don't look too clever.' After about ten minutes of examination, Dr Stone pronounced, 'I'm pretty certain you've got some sort of virus. You're displaying all the symptoms. You've got a slight temperature and your throat is very sore. Obviously all the singing doesn't help that, especially the way you bawl it out.'

Poddy wiped his brow with a paper handkerchief. 'Well, I'm not exactly Pavarotti, but I'm feeling absolutely wiped out, doc, like a cowing corpse.'

'Well, there are just two concerts to go. I'll give you a vitamin and mineral tonic and something to bring your temperature down. Then you've just got to rest and relax as much as possible to get through the remaining shows.'

'Yeah, it's bad enough feeling like crap warmed up, but having that irritating little Mexican hash around is a major ball-ache. I'd like to ram his stupid sombrero up his arse and pull it out of his gob.'

'But I hear he's a musical legend.'

'And a legendary arsehole!'

Biffo propped himself up on two soft pillows and relaxed in bed in his large private room at St Tracey's Hospital. Two doting nurses were hanging on his every request.

'Now, Mr Biffo, we've got you a nice pot of tea with lightly buttered toast, real English style. Is that OK, honey?'

The other nurse provided two newspapers. 'And these are from England, *The Times* and the *Mirror* – they were flown in today. I can also get you some English magazines later, honey. And that book on Pol Pot you wanted will be delivered this afternoon.'

Biffo looked completely relaxed. There was even the vestige of a smile across his cadaverous features. The first nurse spoke calmly. 'The doctors are very pleased with your progress. In fact, I can tell you they're delighted. There's no lasting damage. You could well be home next week and you'll be able to take your dogs for a nice walk. All you have to do is change your diet a little bit, so no more of your British bacon butties.'

Biffo actually smiled broadly. The second nurse spread the newspapers across the bed. 'I bet you miss playing with your band.'

Biffo burst into laughter. 'I do, I must confess... like a hole in the head. Much as I'm enjoying it here, I'm starting to feel a lot better and can't wait to go home.'

Biffo sank back again into the pillows and sipped his tea. He had just started to peruse the front page of *The Times* when the bedside phone rang.

'Hello, Sylvie… Yeah, I feel great… Honestly, I've never felt better… A secluded old farmhouse in Dovedale… ? What, you've paid the deposit already, without me seeing… You're sure it's absolutely perfect and just what we want… South-facing with views over the valley, that sounds fantastic… Not a soul nearby, that's even better… It sounds wonderful… Yeah, Lambert and Perkin will just love it… We can get away from those nosey fookin' neighbours… By the way, while I'm here, can you order that new biography of Nelson and the one on Papa Doc?'

Back at their hotel in Phoenix, the Dogs were preparing for the penultimate gig of their brief but exhausting US tour. Although shattered, the Dogs were a success; more than that, they were now a worldwide phenomenon. Their album was now a best-seller everywhere from Australia to Albania and Zaire to Zanzibar. Their bank balances were healthy and their record company was ecstatic, but the four Dogs themselves had been reduced to three very unhappy hounds.

Fiona Clamp wasn't much happier, either. She was frustrated, and when 'Twin Peaks' was frustrated she was like a storm in a double D-cup. She couldn't get any access to the band and was struggling to add to her portfolio of Dogs' tales. She sat smouldering over a large latte and chocolate muffin in the corner of the coffee lounge of the Dogs' hotel. For a moment she was torn between sinking her fangs into the muffin or investigating the ringing emitting from her handbag. She set down her muffin with a sigh and plumbed the depths of her large Louis Vuitton bag to try to ferret out her mobile. Amid curses she dug out bottles of perfume, lipsticks, tampons, paper handkerchiefs, keys, gloves, scarves, notebooks, pens, bars of chocolate, a digital tape recorder, a camera and a small furry bear. At last she located the phone and pressed the green button, only to hear Dick Rodger's strained, insipid voice. 'Look, Fi, I was in a board meeting this morning and Lord Rotherham was there. He thinks the trail has gone a bit cold; we could do with another Dogs' lead story. And, as he's the owner, I think it sounds like a good idea.'

'A Dogs' lead: that's a good idea, Dick. What the fuck do you and Lord Shitface think I've provided for the past six months? Obituaries and WI tea party reviews?'

Rodger was used to this. 'No, Fi, it's just that you've done so well, we could do with something to keep the pot boiling...'

Fiona Clamp was spitting hot fur balls at that one. 'You've got a short memory, Dick, and a short dick too probably, although I can't imagine a single man, woman or beast on the planet willing to find out. Perhaps you've forgotten that little double exclusive of Biffo telling that pompous Yank reporter to fuck off and then the revelations about Smudger being bisexual. They weren't Parish Pump fillers: they were bloody massive global stories. In fact, they were bigger than the shitting Milky Way. We got them first, thanks entirely to me, and sales of your pissy little paper shot through the fucking roof.'

'Yes, I know, Fi, you've done a great job.'

'A great job? A great fucking job? Look, Dick, don't give me that patronising crap.'

Fiona was purple-faced, her huge chest heaving up and down like the swell of ocean waves in a perfect storm. Dick would have been seasick if he could see her. Fiona imagined his grey, haunted face at the other end of the phone and suddenly couldn't be bothered to continue battering him. He was no contest and it wasn't his fault anyway. She sighed and spoke in a new and quieter, kinder way to her boss.

'For goodness sake, Dick, tell Lord Rotherham he's got more than his money's worth. I notice the share price has shot up. He should be able to buy another coal shed and a couple of whippets, the toffee-nosed twat. These stories have pushed circulation figures up to a record. You told me that.'

'Yes, I know, Fi; you're a victim of your own success.'

'Yeah, success! Fortunately, that's being recognised over here, even if it isn't back in London. I've been offered a job and more money by the *National Enquirer*. Tell that to Lord Shitface.'

'Now, don't be hasty, Fi.' She could hear the terror in Dick's voice and smiled as he continued. 'You're our number one reporter. You always will be while I'm editor. Lord Rotherham knows that. He'd have my guts for garters if you go.'

'So I can expect a big, fat bonus when I get back. I'm sure Lord Snooty will go for it, aren't you, Dick?'

Fiona was standing with her phone trapped between her shoulder and her ear, with her hands on her hips and her loaded nipples pointing forward. If Dick had been in front of her he'd have been cowering now. Even at several thousand miles' distance he was feeling as if someone was pointing something big and dangerous at his head.

'Well, I'm sure he'll consider it,' he said slowly.

'Consider, conschmidder,' said Fi. 'He can stick it up his arse and let it whistle Dixie for all I care. I'm getting fed up with working for the fucking *Comet* and its soft porn subsidiaries. I'll talk to you later. And Dick, don't let it be a conversation about how much notice I have to give. I'm sure you're getting my drift.'

Dick was and said so, before putting the phone down shakily. After a few deep breaths, Dick Rodger did what he always did at times of stress: he studied the artwork of his group's new magazine, *All Bum and Bust*. It was the equivalent of a child comforting itself with a dummy.

Fiona Clamp snapped her mobile shut, and was beginning to cram the pyramid of objects on the table back into her bag when she felt a hand softly pat her on the head.

She turned around like lightning to be confronted by Smudger. With him was the young man from the black-and-white photos acquired by Jerry Ziebahrt. The boy was now a good-looking man in his early forties.

'Hi, Fi, this is Rupert. Mind if we sit with you?'

Fi said nothing. This had caught her unawares and she didn't like being caught off-guard.

'It appears you're a little aggravated. Something bothering you, babe?'

Fiona recovered herself. 'No, no, of course not.'

As they all sat together Fiona was still a little embarrassed and flustered. Smudger's perma-grin was wider than usual. 'Fi, it's time for a little introduction. This is my beloved son, Rupert.'

Fiona staggered and forced out a reply. 'Of course, I mean, as soon as you sat down together – I mean... the likeness.'

Rupert laughed heartily. Smudger tried to put Fiona at ease. 'Look, babe, don't worry. We've got a story to tell and you've got the means to spread it worldwide. "I'm the man who sells the greatest stories in the world." Don't I always look after you, Fi?'

Fiona stared ahead. What an idiot. 'I'm just so sorry. I can't believe it. It was so stupid. I got things so wrong with those photos.'

Rupert was still laughing.

'Don't worry,' said Smudger. 'I can assure you that Rupie and I were very amused by the story. So Fi, you can make it good by telling the real truth. Got your little notebook handy?'

Smudger told the tale, reinforced by nods of affirmation from Rupert.

'I had a relationship with Rupie's mum, Lorelli, in the late sixties. She was a very talented singer. A wonderful chick. Great mum. We produced Rupert. When we split up, Lorelli married a Texan oil magnate called Jeb Cash.

'He was a real weird guy. The deal was, strange as it may seem, that Rupert was to be known as Cash's son, otherwise he wouldn't gain his inheritance. I was only allowed a few secret meetings arranged by Lorelli. At first I pretended I was his uncle. Then, when Rupert was five, Lorelli tragically died in a car smash. So he was brought up by a host of nannies and governesses, rarely saw Jeb Cash and went to a succession of boarding schools.'

Smudger had come into the room convinced he could tell the story without too much emotion, but he was starting to choke up. He lowered his head and Rupert reached out and put an affectionate hand on his shoulder. Fiona was busy jotting down Smudger's tale verbatim in immaculate shorthand, but she could see the affection between the two.

'So what happened next, Rupert?' she asked quietly.

'Well, to keep it short, I was shown documentation when I was about twelve that my favourite uncle was in fact my dad.'

'God, that must have been weird?'

'Well, maybe, but I was delighted. My 'uncle' had been the only person close to me. I was overjoyed he was my pa, but we had to keep it a close secret. At school I hardly ever saw my… Well, I suppose you'd call Jeb Cash my stepdad. I didn't dislike him at all. Throughout this time I kept in close contact with my real dad and my step-pa. Although we didn't see each other very often we did get on OK, but it was always a bit of a distant relationship. Not like the one with my real pa. We used to meet up in all sorts of places. I know his life has been a bit chaotic and colourful to say the least, but he's a very supportive and fun guy. The amazing thing is that for all he's supposed to have been through, he's the fittest man you'll ever meet. I couldn't beat him in a race around the block.'

Rupert chuckled to himself and then looked wistful as he remembered another story from his past. 'There was one thing I did enjoy about my stepdad and that was trying to find him at his various residences. He had this place near Austin that made the Southfork Ranch look like a shack. Then there was his colonial house in Key West. That was my favourite. He also had a plush apartment overlooking Central Park and this amazing house up in Nebraska, complete with bears on the loose. He had staff at all the houses, but he was never at the same one more than a day or two. I rarely caught up with him. There was one particular mobile phone that my stepdad sometimes answered, although it was usually on message, nine times out of ten.'

He paused, deep in thought. 'Anyway, that's all over now. As you may have read in the papers, he died yesterday. I suppose no one will really miss him and there'll be lots of hyenas after any bits and pieces he may have left behind. But I'll always thank him for giving me a big allowance, which helped me to get into Harvard to study law. After I graduated I worked for a New York firm and then set up my own practice, specialising in the oil business. It was about this time I met my wife, Jemima. She's a very committed family lawyer, so we don't have any kids.' Again, the regretful pause.

Smudger patted Rupert rather too heartily on the shoulder. 'You see, Fiona, my son's a very bright boy.'

Fiona Clamp took a sip of her coffee. 'I'm sorry to hear about your stepfather passing away.'

'Don't be – he wasn't a real father anyway. He was only ever interested in making money, not making relationships work. He was always working, spending his days in chauffeur-driven limos, private jets and boardrooms. No wonder I could never get hold of him.'

Smudger looked at Fiona, who was showing rather too much interest in this aspect of the story, and decided to jump in. 'So Rupie is selling all his stepdad's oil interests and property, and he and Jemima are moving to Britain.'

Rupert's broad smile was a perfect and equally disarming copy of Smudger's. 'You see, although my stepdad didn't know how to deal with kids, he still wanted me to be his son and heir. If the identity of my real dad had been exposed, he'd have been furious and I'd have lost my inheritance – millions, well, nearly a billion dollars. It's all been quite a crazy charade, but I realised the score from an early age. I wanted to prove I could make it on my own, so I studied hard to get my law degree and I've made a few bucks along the way. I'll still work as a lawyer in London and so will Jemima.'

Smudger held up his hands. '"Ground control to Major Tom." Fi, that's enough. You tell all our tale, but just don't reveal how much Rupie has inherited – please.'

Fiona nodded. 'Can I get some pics of you two together?'

'That's no problem, if it's OK with Rupie.'

'No worries, dad; it's family snapshot time.'

Rupert and Smudger struck up a series of comical poses. Fiona laughed aloud as she clicked her tiny digital camera. She was surprising herself. She liked these two and there was no way she was going to try to stitch them up. This was a good news story.

A few minutes later Smudger and Rupert left Fiona in the lounge. She jabbed speed dial on her phone.

'Dick, I'm just going to file yet another world exclusive. The trail has hotted up a bit. The pot's boiling again. It's called Smudger and son, Dog and pup. Tell Lord Snooty Shitface that I'm expecting a big bonus for this one or else I'm off. Don't forget!' And with that, Fiona Clamp triumphantly snapped her phone shut, buried it in her bag and ordered a treble gin and tonic.

Chapter Twenty-One

Brian 'Streaky' Bacon stormed into the Dogs' dressing room in Phoenix after another acid interrogation from Arabella and hurled his mobile phone against a wall. No one there was in a fit state to react. Poddy was slumped in a corner; his face, normally ruddy in complexion, was pasty white, his eyes expressionless and embedded in even darker rims. In the bright light he looked to have two black eyes.

Smudger was talking animatedly to Oops in the corridor. They hugged before he entered the dressing room. Poddy looked up. 'Thank God it's you. I thought it was going to be that little Mexican twat. I've never believed in love at first sight, but he's convinced me you can hate someone as soon as you flamin' well meet them.'

Smudger pushed his black leather Stetson further back. 'Yeah, I haven't taken to him either.'

Streaky was oblivious to the mood of the others. He picked up his battered mobile. 'Arabella is absolutely paranoid. She keeps accusing me of sleeping with a succession of women.'

He sat deep in thought and spoke quietly to Poddy and Smudger. 'Although I was uneasy about the whole thing at first, what with my career in the bank and all that, I must admit it's been fabulous; well, financially fabulous, that is. But now, after six months with hardly a break, what have we got? Biffo's had a heart attack. My marriage needs a bit of mending, and my two sons sound a little estranged. I don't know what they think of me now. You're really suffering, Poddy. I must say I've never seen you look so poorly.'

'Yeah, thanks for the encouragement.'

'No, I mean it. And even you, Smudger, look tired out. Now we'll all be insulted by that arrogant little bastard.'

On cue, the door burst open and in strode Buzz Diablo in a fringed white suede suit, covered with rhinestones. Buzz was issuing instructions as he walked in. 'Bass man, just remember you take your lead from me. Just watch the way I work. Try and follow, gringo. The problem is, I'm a little too good for you. You other two guys, you'll learn more in a night playing with me than you will in a year in a two-bit band. Mr Piano Man, one day you can play some real jazz, but you're light years away yet, buddy. You've got to get the feel, the tempo, the timing.'

Buzz pointed at Poddy. 'And if you can sing in key tonight, boy, that would be nice for a change. You're as flat as one of my old mama's tortillas.'

Poddy tensed and looked as if he might get up and thump Buzz, but he was too ill to do more than stare back for a moment and say, 'Why don't you go and sit on a fucking cactus.'

Buddy Peabody arrived just in time to apply some rapid diplomacy. 'Don't worry, Buzz, no offence meant. It's dad's peculiar British wit. One of those things that I know you guys find hard to get used to. Just a bit of fun. Anyway, lads, everything's all right. We're set for a great evening. There's a big crowd out there and quite some atmosphere. We've sold a massive amount of merchandise. They can't wait.' He kept talking until it was too late for the band to think about anything except the gig ahead.

In the middle of the first track of the Dogs' set, Buzz put in an unexpected and convoluted drum solo, setting a marker for the rest of the show. He spent the night interjecting with unexpected drum rolls and solos, much to Poddy's growing fury. It was becoming a bit of a showcase for Buzz Diablo, with the Dogs in a supporting role. Even the crowd was getting restless. People had paid to hear the Dogs and not ten-minute drum solos from the seventy-two-year-old Mexican musician. The band finished with an encore, but the audience was a little subdued and less enthusiastic than at the other venues. At the finish, Buzz Diablo pushed his way to the front of the stage, threw some drumsticks into the crowd, took off his sombrero and gave a succession of theatrical bows. Poddy, Smudger and Streaky were already heading for the dressing room. Poddy collapsed on a sofa in exhaustion. He couldn't even raise the energy to curse Buzz, who joined them a few minutes later still in band leader mode.

'Told you guys just to follow me, right. We've got to tighten a few things up. Singer, if we can call you that, you were flat on those first two songs. Bass man, you've got to work with me a bit closer, get that feel. Mr Piano Man, you've got a lot to learn. You'd never get into one of my bands. Imagine you playing with the Count or the Duke. It's the timing, that goes for all you gringos. Now I've got to sort out a show for President Vladimir Putin in Russia. Now ain't that something – wouldn't take you guys with me, ha! I've played for every Russian president. I'll tell ya, I'll be taking some real players to Russia. See you boys at the Hollywood Bowl tomorrow. It'll be your last gig with a legend. Just make sure you get in that siesta beforehand. You boys sure look whacked – and lay off the tequila.'

He swaggered out of the dressing room without a backward glance. For a few seconds Poddy, Smudger and Streaky looked at the door wordlessly. The silence was broken by Smudger, who, for the first time, lost his cool and burst into an angry rant. 'That little bastard is trading on our name and talent. We could have got a session drummer in just as good as him without the fucking attitude. I know plenty in LA. He's not all he's cracked up to be anyway. I'll tell you guys, I'm not playing another gig, or even coming within spitting distance of that short-arsed little turd. Never again. That's it, guys, finito. "It's all over now baby blue".'

Poddy was slumped in the corner, looking like a scarecrow with a face moulded out of putty. He stared into space for a while before starting to speak. 'Y'know, this started as a fantasy. I loved every moment at first. Bloody adored it. Now we're all fabulously rich, but we've earned it. We've been on the go, recording, doing concerts, press conferences and all the rest of it without a break for months. Usually we work from dawn to cowing dusk. I used to have Friday afternoons, Saturday and Sunday off, go to a match, enjoy a few pints, put my feet up, watch TV, even take the missus out for a meal. I don't think I've got a cowing drop left in the tank to do another gig and any which way I'm not working with that Mexican bandit again. That's definite. He can fuck off back to Tijuana or wherever he comes from. I looked at my diary and we've had three days off in about six months, and most of those days we spent on the phone talking about this or that.' He caught Streaky's eye. 'Well, mainly talking about THAT in Streaky's case.'

'I've never been so insulted in all my life,' said Streaky. 'No, not with you, Poddy; I can still take a joke. But I can't take some silly little drummer trying to tell me how to play piano. Why, I've played classical recitals to big audiences. I'm a concert pianist. The more I think about it, I can't wait to get tomorrow over. I just can't be bothered to even speak to our conceited little Mexican friend. If we could fly back now I'd be bloody delighted.'

Poddy butted in. 'Now there's a thought. At this very moment, I want a long holiday, a long rest, and a pint of Marston's. Well, several pints of Marston's and a few footy matches. Why don't we just go?'

Buddy Peabody and Dr Stone walked in. Buddy was totally unaware of how the group was feeling. He was carrying a large folder and was focused on the task in hand.

'I've checked through a lot of things, and in all the hurly burly of the last few weeks there's just one thing I've overlooked, fellas. I hope you'll forgive me. I forgot to get you to sign the contracts for this tour, the forthcoming European tour and new album. I know you all agreed to it verbally, but I need you to sign on the dotted line.'

Poddy suddenly looked like a new man. He laughed and tried to jump up. 'Well, that's it! That's our get-out!'

He was exhilarated and shouting. 'We've been saved. We can forget the final cowing concert. We haven't signed a contract to do the fucking thing – it's cowin' fantastic.'

Dr Stone interrupted. 'Well, I would recommend that you don't do the final concert anyway. You're just not fit to carry out any concert or any activity, so sit down, Poddy. After my examination, I think you need at least three weeks' rest. That's how long I'd sign you off for, right now. You can't perform as the Dogs with only two fit members of the band.'

'Well, there's no way I want to play another concert anyway,' said Streaky, 'so between Dr Stone and the unsigned contract I think we might just prevent a load of problems and unpleasantness.'

Smudger was smiling. 'We're watertight. We haven't signed

the contract and, anyway, two members of the band are unfit for work and can't play, and I'll repeat I'm not going on stage again with that little Mexican runt and that's final.'

Poddy clenched his fist in a gesture of solidarity. 'Yeah, I'm ready to barbecue the little sod's Chihuahua.'

Buddy was the only one looking worried. 'It's all right for you three, but Radische will kill me. I have to play piggy in the middle. But if that's what you really want, let's see if we can sort something out, although we haven't exactly got a lot of time. I just need a chance to talk to God and Oops about this. I need help to find a simple solution.'

'Yeah, there's a very simple solution,' said Poddy. 'We ain't doing the cowing concert. Buzz can bore the arse off the audience by playing a three-hour jazz drum solo. I, for one, won't be there to see it.'

After the meeting Smudger sounded out Oops. 'We've gotta talk, babe, but "a little less conversation a little more action". Let's share a bottle of red.'

They found a softly upholstered velvet corner of the hotel bar. Smudger made a sign to a waiter. 'Hey cat! I'll have a bottle of that Barolo, and a couple of glasses.'

Smudger joined Oops and when the wine arrived he poured two large measures. Before he could start to speak she pre-empted his opening address. 'Yes, I know, you hate that little Mexican git. Join the club, who doesn't? Even God never realised what a self-centred, egotistical, conceited little braggart he is.'

'He's a shit.'

'Very succinct. We're all aware of how difficult the situation is at the moment. Biffo is still recovering in hospital but is doing very well. Poddy is ill; he looks absolutely dreadful. Believe me, we're moving heaven and earth to try and sort something out to postpone the final concert at the Hollywood Bowl. But the problem is there're quite a few spin-offs from this concert. We don't want it to go ahead with you all in this state. So come on now, relax and enjoy your wine.'

Smudger was still uncharacteristically hyper. 'I will, I will but... See, babe, I have to point out that we never signed a contract for these concerts.'

'OK. Don't worry, you're safe. I'm on your side.'

Smudger visibly unwound as she said that. 'Here, let me top up your glass. "Red, red wine," and all the latest research says it's good for you, babe.'

'That's more like my boy.'

'Your boy, eh, Oops?'

He leaned forward and kissed her before she could stop him. Not that she had any intention of doing that. She responded to the touch of his lips. They were like teenagers, heads virtually welded together in a full-on, passionate and lengthy face-chewing snog. They pulled apart like two suction pads being separated. Smudger whispered, 'Never knew you cared, babe.'

'Yes, I suppose I do, you old dog. Anyway, I've decided to throw in the towel with Jet Records.'

'What, after all these years, with a pension, a long service medal, luncheon vouchers and a watch?'

'Yes, I'm not that keen on Brett Radische. We didn't get on from the day God brought him into the firm. I must admit he's very efficient, but he's a short-tempered little sod. Not exactly full of bonhomie.'

'So what are you gonna do?'

'Well, I've already made enquiries. I've got quite a little business portfolio already. I'm going to do some work with God and a few bits and pieces for other companies and magazines. It looks very exciting, my new life as a freelance.'

Smudger pushed back the brim of his hat. 'You know, I had my best times as a freelance musician. I remember doing Mondays and Tuesdays working on recordings with The Doors, The Dead and Love. Then I did some blues sessions in Chicago on Wednesdays and Thursdays; sometimes I finished up jamming in all sorts of smoky clubs. Then at the weekends I played here, there and everywhere. I gigged with Santana, Starship, Lynyrd Skynyrd and Little Feat. I was "just making a few bucks. Sort of have bass, will travel". Best days of my life, babe. I've been thinking...'

'That's a new concept for you,' teased Oops.

'No, I really have. You know with Rupie going to Britain, I'm going to follow. Gonna set up a studio somewhere and do a lot of session work just for fun. Maybe do a bit of teaching bass and guitar. Maybe one day we can own a "mansion on the hill". You can light the fire, babe.'

'Wasn't that Crosby, Stills, Nash and Young?'

'That was in the days – didn't I tell you – when it nearly became Crosby, Stills, Nash, Young and Smith?'

'You've only told me that twice… this week. It's your favourite story, along with how you taught Elvis to play the harmonica. Or harp, before you correct me.'

Smudger took no notice of her gentle teasing; he was in full nostalgic flow. 'Yeah, I might look for a place in the country. Maybe back in Derbyshire. It's England's green and pleasant land, babe, it's really beautiful. Reminds me of Elgar. I could get a gym fixed up and grow some crops. With all my contacts it wouldn't be difficult to get a studio rigged up and record a few sessions. Find myself a rock'n'roll band, do a little writing and play a little cricket.'

'Cricket? You play cricket?'

'Yep, sure thing. I used to play at school, played for the county under-fifteen team. Many years ago we started this Hollywood cricket team and played a few times a year.'

'So who was in that?'

'Well, at one time we got Rod Stewart playing, with Keith Moon keeping wicket. Eric Clapton likes a game, Mick Jagger turned out a few times and so did Bob Willis.'

'Bob Willis? What band was he in?'

'No, he was a real cricketer, a former England captain.'

'But aren't you a bit old for this?'

'You're never too old for rock'n'roll or cricket. It's like swimming or playing the bass, babe, or like sex. You never lose it.'

Oops gulped a large mouthful of red wine.

The next morning Brett Radische called a meeting at a hotel in Hollywood. He was joined by his assistant Bentley Gardner, Buddy Peabody and Oops. Radische was a diminutive man, with a shaven head, dark rodent eyes and a fierce, impatient demeanour. Whereas his predecessor Godfrey Vanderbloom had been charming, conciliatory and democratic, Radische was curt, overbearing and dictatorial. He started the proceedings by berating a waiter. 'Hey, fella, this coffee's not hot enough and it tastes stale. Bring us some more – and some cookies, pronto.'

After the waiter left Radische began a fierce attack on those left. 'So why haven't these guys signed the contract for the tour, that's what I want to know. From what I've seen so far, this operation is going as good as the I-raq war.'

Bentley Gardner, a silver-haired veteran of the US music business, just shrugged his shoulders. Buddy Peabody butted in. 'It was just one of those things that got overlooked. OK, it happens, but we've agreed the contract.'

That just made Radische all the more irate. 'Great. You've verbally agreed the contract. That makes me feel so much better. Who witnessed it? Jesus Christ and his disciples? Cos that's the only way we'll make that stick.'

Buddy coughed and started to sweat. 'Well, it was just sort of roughly agreed by me and the members of the band.'

'Roughly agreed – what does that mean? Were the guys all definitely agreed on the contract or not?'

Buddy was squirming uneasily in his seat. It was like a courtroom examination.

'Well I think they were OK with it, but we were so busy with recordings, concerts, appearances and the like that we didn't have much time—'

'What, no time to put four signatures on a goddamn piece of paper? Look, there's just this one gig to go. Let's see that out and have a meeting to get the whole shebang sorted for the next tour and album.'

Oops boldly interrupted Radische. 'Look, Brett, there's no way they can complete tonight's gig. As you know, Charlie Bear's had a heart attack and Lenny Peabody's suffering from exhaustion and a severe viral infection. There's no way he can sing. We're going to have to cancel tonight, and,' she paused, 'to be honest, now they know there's no contract they just won't play.'

Radische looked like a man who'd just taken a bite of a burger and discovered half a mouse. 'Hey, these guys agreed verbally to fulfil these concerts. As far as I'm concerned that's like swearing on their mothers' lives. They performed OK in Phoenix with that Buzz Diablo. We're only asking for one finale at the Hollywood Bowl. They've agreed to it; they'll have to do the goddamn thing.

Then they can fly back to England for tea and scones or whatever else you Limeys eat. Is that understood?'

Oops continued to argue. 'There are only two of the four fit to play. If Mick Jagger and Keith Richards were ill, the Rolling Stones would cancel a gig. The Dogs are not the Dogs without Charlie Bear and Lenny Peabody. The crowd have paid to see the band at their best. Just cancel the gig due to illness and give the crowd a refund. It's perfectly simple.'

'Yeah, to someone with your grasp of business, but we can't do that. This is the most important concert; there's a lot riding on this one; it has to go ahead. We're doing a live DVD and already projected world sales will be the biggest ever. It'll be fabulous for the Christmas market, so don't waste my time talking about what's simple or not. What's simple is with no concert we've got no profit, so, Buddy boy, just go and tell your dad one more gig, OK? I'm sure with a bit of medical help he can manage that. That's settled.'

Brett Radische was already standing up as a sign that the meeting was terminated.

Buddy Peabody rushed back to inform the three remaining members of the band of the new MD's decision. They all met up in Poddy's hotel room. The Dogs looked strained and tense. Buddy tried one more appeal. 'Guys, there's just one more concert; you can do it on automatic pilot. Dad, it's just one final effort, then we can go home. Look, you're all set up for life; the records have made millions. Then we can take a break and thrash out where we go from here. We'll lighten the workload and build in lots of leisure time for the new tour and album. They can't take anything away from you. We agreed that first contract. It's paid out millions and there's more millions to be made.'

Poddy gasped, 'Look, son, I just can't do another gig. My voice is going, I'm absolutely cowing knackered and I couldn't bear playing with that Mexican bastard. I'd have to kill him, but I haven't even got the energy for that.'

Streaky nodded in agreement. 'I've had enough, too. I'm not going to be insulted again by that arrogant, conceited, obnoxious, self-opinionated, over-rated, rude, short-arse little twassock and that's it.'

Smudger concurred. 'Sorry, Buddy, it's unanimous – I'm out too.'

Buddy turned to his father. 'Dad, I know you're not well, but see sense – there's only one gig and a few hours to go. It's not asking for much.'

'It's too much. As I keep repeating, we've not signed a contract, so that's it. We're free to go. A car's picking us up at seven for Los Angeles airport. They'll just have to refund the money and issue an apology. That way nobody really loses out, apart from Jet making a cowing fortune from our efforts on a live DVD. Whose side are you on? I didn't bring you up to be a money-grabbing vulture like Radische.'

The effort made him gasp for air. Buddy was furious at being ticked off like a schoolboy but bit his tongue. He looked at his father and could see he was ill. His anger subsided. 'Yeah, you're right. We've made plenty. Let's tell Radische to stuff it.'

Olivia Olga Ponsonby-Smart was in defiant mood. She picked up her mobile and dialled through to Brett Radische.

'Brett, the concert's off. I know there's only three hours to go… Well, that's your hard luck… We've already had one near-fatality on stage with Charlie Bear, I don't think we can afford another one, can we… Frankly I don't give a flying fuck what you think. You can sue all you like, but they haven't even signed a contract to do this work… I don't think I'm getting through to you, and very few people do it appears. I'll repeat it one more time for the hard of understanding: the concert is off tonight… And to you, too. It's been nice working with you, Brett; go and polish your head.'

Oops yelped with delight as she finished the call and muttered to herself, 'Six-love, six-love, a result.'

Buzz Diablo had been taking his afternoon siesta on a sofa in the plush dressing rooms at the Hollywood Bowl. He was now ready for the concert. He snapped his fingers and called over a member of the road crew. 'Be careful when you're setting up my equipment; it's all custom-made and specially tuned and set up for me.'

The roadie turned to move away, but Buzz called him back. 'Hey, boy, there's a few other things I need. I want three large towels by my kit, and three half-litre bottles of ice cold mineral water, and I mean ice cold.'

'So is this your last appearance with the Dogs?'

'I think it will be. It's hard playing with guys like this who are not quite up to the job. It's not like playing real jazz. It's just so simple. When I get those gringos together tonight I'm gonna try and whip them into some kind of shape. You know the big problem, they need a bit of schooling from old Buzz. They're just a two-bit bar band, who've stumbled on a bit of luck by playing with a legend. Now ain't that something. I'll tell ya, if the Duke, the Count, Woody or Ella knew I was playing with this band of deadbeats they'd be turning in their graves. Why, the singer sounds like his tonsils have been peppered with chilli powder. I think he sometimes sings in a different key to the rest of the band. The bass player can't keep time properly and the pianist would be OK for playing organ in church. I'd need a lot of sessions to make something out of those boys. But next week I'm off on a world tour with some real musicians. I'm playing in Russia, China, Japan, Australia and Brazil. Now ain't that something. Seventy-two years old, Buzz Diablo: have sticks will travel. Just mind you look after my kit, boy.'

Buzz Diablo suddenly was silenced by a loudspeaker announcement. 'Owing to illness, tonight's concert by the Dogs is cancelled. Everyone with tickets will get a full refund. Can you please queue in an orderly fashion to get your money back. We are sorry for the inconvenience.'

By this time nearly 80,000 people were packed into the Hollywood Bowl waiting for the concert to start. The late announcement took everyone by surprise. The crowd howled in displeasure.

At seven thirty that evening a long, black limousine with blacked-out windows swept around to the front entrance of the hotel. The three remaining members of the Dogs, Buddy Peabody and Oops, incognito in hats and dark glasses, got on board. By 8.30 p.m. they had checked in at Los Angeles airport. At the same time as the crowd were filing out of the concert venue, Poddy, Smudger, Streaky, Buddy and Oops were enjoying a brandy and coffee in the first-class lounge. Poddy had recaptured a little joie de vivre. Although he'd nearly lost his voice, he raised his glass and croaked out, 'Here's to our mate Buzz's three-hour drum solo, and to Brett Radische: up yours.'

The Dogs had gone walkies.

Chapter Twenty-Two

With thousands of disgruntled fans still streaming away from the Hollywood Bowl, Brett Radische called an emergency meeting with his number two, Bentley Gardner, and May Moon, a young, whiz-kid lawyer employed by Jet Records.

Radische thumped the table with a clenched fist. 'Just one more goddamn gig to go. That was all, for Chrissake. Goddamn chicken-livered Limeys!'

Gardner, a veteran of the music and entertainment business and of Radische's grumpy outbursts, tried a more conciliatory and sympathetic approach. 'The doc did say there were good reasons for calling off the concert.'

Radische snorted impatiently. 'Valid goddamn reasons. Right. So the singer was a bit tired. I'm goddamn tired. The sonofabitch. They could have done one more gig. And we've missed out on the live DVD. That was set to gross twenty million. With Buzz Diablo on board we were guaranteed two different markets and mammoth earnings. Absolute mega mammoth, for Chrissake. That would have been one goddamn profitable piece of merchandise, millions of bucks. And they were kinda tired!' He screamed the last sentence, banging one fist into the palm of his other hand. Gardner was reminded of an unsettling news reel he'd seen of Hitler at some Nazi rally or other.

May Moon was just four years out of Harvard, but already an experienced intellectual property lawyer and a smart cookie. She knew who the boss was and she wasn't about to upset him. 'Brett, we're caught between Iraq and Iran here. Not a happy place to be, but let's see what we can do. Yes, they've got grounds not to play if a doctor says a guy isn't fit to play. It's like any work situation, but let's look at those unsigned contracts for this tour. We can—'

Radische hammered the table again. 'That's down to the banjo players running this place before me. All that gentleman's agreement shit. British baloney. Jolly jam scones and cups of fucking tea. Come on, May, get us out of this.'

May put on a look of someone thinking hard to find an answer to a difficult problem, but her sharp, Harvard-educated brain had long ago come up with a solution. She just wanted to remind Radische how brilliant she was.

'Well, they've completed the obligations of their only existing contract, but, as I understand it, they said they would do a European tour and another album. That's the way to go. Chase them for that tour and album. Plenty of people heard them say they'd do it. We can still come out on top.'

Radische broke in again. 'And there's that live DVD too. I'm gonna hunt these guys down and they'll honour their agreement or they won't have long to enjoy all that money they've stolen from us.'

Bentley Gardner coughed loudly. He could see Radische was losing it. If he was allowed to rant on, he'd do his Robert de Niro act and Gardner had seen that enough times not to want to see it again. The man was a prick. 'That may be difficult. There doesn't seem to be any agreement, let alone a contract. Anyway, rumour has it they're already on a plane back to the UK, claiming they've retired.'

Radische roared. 'Retired! Goddamn retired. We'll see about that. Their asses are mine!'

The Dogs' entourage was reduced to six refugees from the tour, split into three pairs sprawled well apart in business class on the Airbus bound for Heathrow. Poddy sat near the front with Dr Chris Stone, who had administered a mild sedative to help the tired old dog through the flight. The two had grown close on the last three days of the tour. Poddy looked grim, gaunt and ghostly, but was starting to recover his natural optimism.

'Tell you, Doc, any which way, once this cowing plane gets airborne, I'll be as happy as a slug in a cauliflower. First thing I'm going to do when I get back is have a nice pot of tea, then a pint of pedigree. One after t'other! Then I'm going to watch every cowing footy match on telly from the Premiership to the Conference and the Derbyshire Pork Butchers' Sunday League. Oh, and I'm going to take Barbara out for the biggest bloody banquet we've ever had. Then, in case I forget, there are more than a few nights out with me mates at the Ferret and Bicycle in the pipeline. Imagine owning your own local. Now there's a thought, or, as that Mexican twat would say, "now ain't that something?"' He could even smile when he thought of Buzz, the memories fading as the distance between them grew. 'I'm going to the next Derby County match. Might even buy them a decent striker, as a gift. Do you know something, Doc, I miss the pest control business. Wrestling with rats, mice, squirrels, moles, wasps and cockroaches is a doddle compared to the music business. Well, not exactly wrestle with them, but no one knows more about those critters than me. I've got a lot of respect for them, which is more than I can say for pests and vermin like Radische and his like.'

Poddy hardly paused for breath. He was happier than he'd been in ages. He continued in a softer voice and with more of a warm mutter. 'Pints of peddy, a really good curry, toast and chunky marmalade, loads of footy, Barbara's apple crumble with thick custard…' And he then stretched out and fell asleep.

Smudger and Oops were separated from Poddy and Dr Stone by two empty rows. They sipped champagne and cuddled and giggled like teenagers on a first date. At the end of the runway Smudger burst into song. '"Commencing countdown engines on".'

Oops laughed out aloud. 'I knew that was coming.'

Smudger crooned softly in her ear, '"I'm leaving on a jet plane, …". Tell you what, babe, I probably won't. I'm back to Blighty for good, especially with my boy based in England.'

Oops prodded him in the ribs. 'Well, you probably won't be that welcome back in the States. For starters there are a hundred thousand miffed fans still baying for your blood – and Brett Radische, the man with a name like an angry vegetable and an intellect to match.'

Smudger grinned and burst into song again. 'He looks like a bespectacled turnip and I never liked turnips, preferred Swedes. Hey, we're heading for Staines.'

'Heading for *stains*?'

'Yeah, Staines, babe. Staines, Middlesex: it's by Heathrow.'

'Oh, I'm with you, big boy.'

'We need some good vintage red, babe.'

Smudger pressed the button to summon the flight attendant.

'"Ground control to Major Tom… ". I'm sorry, Major Thomasina.'

The flight attendant smiled patronisingly. Smudger was too happy to care.

'What can I get you?'

'Babe, can you find the best vintage bottle of red in the house, something like a Claret, Châteauneuf du Pape or Barolo.'

'We've got all of those, sir.'

'OK. Let's start with the Claret.' Smudger turned to Oops. "Seems like it's going to be a very enjoyable flight. I remember the time I was helping out this band. We were just whizzing around the States in a Lear Jet full of cocaine. High in the sky, babe. Just crazy. I flew from LA to Seattle in this big transport plane once, doing this big jam session with a few pals. It was the mile-high band. Jim Morrison was singing, I was playing this string bass, Keith Moon was hammering away on a makeshift drum kit made up of crates, boxes and cans, and Steve Ray Vaughan was strumming away on a battered Spanish guitar. I once flew from Frisco to New Orleans on a charter plane for a blues concert. I was in the band backing Blind Willie, Big Willie and Boxcar Willie—'

Oops sniggered.

'Sounds like the three willies tour. You must have fitted in well with that crowd.'

'I also played organ on those gigs.'

'I bet you did.'

Two rows further back Buddy Peabody sat with Streaky. Both were subdued. Buddy swigged from a can of lager. Streaky sipped a mineral water. Buddy broke a long spell of silence.

'Hope my dad's OK. He certainly will be when he checks his bank balance.' Buddy was feeling guilty at having had a go at his father, but felt a little hard done to himself.

'He'll be fine,' said Streaky. 'He's a tough old dog… I mean old sod. I've known him since secondary school, long before you came on the scene. He was three years above me, but even in those days everyone looked up to him. He was seen as a leader.

You know, we're all completely knackered. Do you realise that we've been going non-stop for about nine months without a break? Long hours, long days, working at night. The schedule would have knocked out a twenty-year-old, let alone a bunch of over-sixties.'

Buddy looked thoughtful.

'I know. I should have maybe thought about your ages a bit more, but we had to make the most of it. As I said, just look at your bank balance. You of all people should know all about that.'

'Funny you should mention that. The last thing I did in the departure lounge was check my account on the internet. I just couldn't believe it. Got the small matter of a tax bill to pay. That should knock a hole in thirty million. But who cares.'

Buddy smiled broadly.

'There's more to come. We haven't received all the royalties, by any means. There should be a steady supply for years to come, what with all the world sales as well.'

Streaky looked a little uneasy.

'Being so exhausted has meant we've all lost a bit of a grip on reality lately. It's just been a bewildering time when you think about it. One minute we're heading gracefully towards retirement and all of a sudden we're multimillionaires. It's crazy, and I have to say I've had enough of craziness for a while. That's why I'm retiring.'

'Will you still do any playing?'

'Yes, of course. I couldn't give that up, but I'll concentrate on concert stuff. I'm going to have a fabulous grand piano installed at my new house. I'll spend my time playing that – and golf.' He paused to let the idea sink in and then turned to Buddy. 'What will you do?'

'Oh, I've got plans too. I'm going to fit out the most up-to-date, state of the art recording studio in the country and discover and record new bands and musicians. I'm also going to settle down a bit.'

'Well, good for you We're all settled. Well, I hope I will be, if Arabella buries the hatchet.'

'Let's hope it's not in the back of your head.'

Streaky looked startled for a second but then grinned and laughed out loud.

Fiona Clamp slammed shut her hotel room door with the force of a Sumo wrestler on steroids. She slumped on the bed, propped herself up with two plump pillows and calmly dialled a number.

'Good morning, Dick – head – and, before you ask, I've got the complete inside story about the Dogs going walkies – all from an impeccable source.'

'Fantastic. You're a star, Fi. I always knew you hadn't lost it, babe.'

Fi made silent gagging motions as Dick continued his syco-phantic eulogy. 'You're just so fucking dependable. I can't understand—'

'Yeah, yeah. Save it, Dick. Let's talk business.'

'Yes, yes, of course... But tell me, who coughed up all the juicy details?'

'Well, I had a nice surreptitious call from a source close to the band, as we say so often in our lying little rag. Anyway, don't try to push me for an answer, cos I won't tell you. We can go with this as a monster exclusive.'

'Oh, deffo, Fi. So what about Biffa's heart attack? True or false?'

'It's Biffo!'

'Whatever. So what's the story on him and the other one, Paddy. Was he really taken ill or was it too much pop – or popping.'

'He's called Poddy!'

'Yeah, that's the fella. Anyway, the official line from both the Dogs' people and the record company is that the tour was cancelled due to illness, as simple as that.'

'Half true, but not that simple. The band was as knackered as you normally are after ten pints of lager and forty Bensons at that seedy basement club you frequent in Dean Street. They'd had enough and just wanted out. The record company really turned the screw and tried to force them to do that last concert. It was getting really nasty. Then, would you believe it, both sides found out that no contract had ever been signed for the fucking tour, new sodding album, live bastard DVD or a new tossing European tour.'

She could hear Dick's brain whirring round, working out the implications of that.

'So the Dogs, much to the chagrin of Jet Records, just turned tail and headed home. They've each made an estimated thirty million or so from what I can gather. So they don't give a flying fuck about the record company or the fans. They're virtually untouchable. They're all going back to Britain to retire and live off the proceeds. All that stuff pushed out by Jet Records was damage limitation.

'The Dogs are going walkies and Jet Records, especially their new MD Brett Radische, are incandescent with rage, but they can do bugger all about it. Two of the Dogs have been given valid doctor's certificates. They haven't even signed a contract for the tour, so Jet Records have proverbially had their bollocks cut off. I can give you the whole tale.'

It was music to Dick Rodger's ears. The last time he felt this good was when he got the bumper edition of *Big and Bouncy*.

'When are you going to file, Fi?'

'I'm not. At least, I'm not until I get a call back from you after you've spoken to Lord Shitface. I've been offered big bucks to stay over here and work for the *National Enquirer*. They'd like this story for starters.'

Dick coughed into his coffee and dropped fag ash onto his already stained nylon shirt.

'This is like blackmail, Fi.'

'What do you mean, "like blackmail?" It *is* blackmail and you're going to pay up, so stop whining. I've pushed your fucking sales through the roof. It's simple enough. I want to be called Chief Correspondent, I want a one hundred percent pay rise, a company car, clothing allowance and health insurance, otherwise I'm off to pastures new, taking this story and my contacts with me. Call me within the hour or don't bother calling again.'

Fiona Clamp threw down the phone and sank back into the pillows. Five minutes later the shrill ringtone chimed out.

She let it ring for a while. She could imagine Dick sweating profusely and drawing blood from fingernails already bitten down to the quick.

'Hello. Oh, really, Dick? That's nice. How kind of Lord Arse-face. Yes, I'm happy enough – for now. I'll file the story as soon as I get your e-mail detailing that offer and a fax signed by the good

Lord. Yeah, well, that's your problem.'

Fiona Clamp closed her mobile, pushed her laptop to one side and picked up the bedside phone.

'Hi, room service. Can you send me up a chilled bottle of champagne and some chips. No, hang on, that means crisps over here, doesn't it? French fries, a big bowl. That should really hit the spot.'

Chapter Twenty-Three

In a plush apartment in London's Little Venice, Gilbert Winstanley, aka Duke Deckster, and his partner Juliette Nelson-Wellington were relaxing after a long day.

'The Dobermen, Bertie! You must be kidding. I think you're getting a fixation about dogs.'

'Well, I think they're the best band since the Dogs and look how well they did for us. The nation awaits, Jules old girl. After I discovered the Dogs my audience figures hit twelve to thirteen million on some mornings. I'd love that again. As I say, the nation awaits and we await a glass of bubby. Where are you hiding it?'

'I've got a couple of bottles of that Bolly in the fridge and I picked up some fab nibbles from Fortnum & Mason's during my lunch hour. By the way, I found some of that amazing Parma ham you like.'

'Oh, goody. Daddy used to send me tons of the stuff to Eton to put in sandwiches. We used to have midnight feasts in the dorm with Parma ham and cheap Lambrusco. Sedgewick, dear old Sedgie, our housemaster, got to find out about it, and in the end he just joined in. I used to give him a few slices for his kids' luncheon boxes.'

'Oh, you've always been such a benevolent old chap, Bertie.'

He smiled. 'What sort of a day have you had, Jules?'

'Well, pretty busy really. Finalised this communication strategy with a shirt company in Jermyn Street. Then I had a latte and raspberry muffin. Walked up Regent Street and after Fortnum & Mason's went to Selfridges for a few things. Then I had a late lunch at Wolfgang and Luigi's.'

Gilbert removed his round scholarly spectacles and propelled his sound system into action.

'You know, I'm convinced the Dobermen will be another big band launched by the Duke. In fact, after the Dogs and the Dobermen, I just need to unveil a band called the Dachshunds next.'

Lenny Peabody was sitting in his new office extension at home pouring through a heap of correspondence with his wife Barbara.

'That just about ties it all up. A dozen vans with state of the art equipment and three top pest control officers to operate them, right across the Midlands. Yep, it's Peabody's Pest Control by the dozen. The pests roll over, the money rolls in and all I have to do is pick and choose any jobs that take my fancy.'

Barbara smiled knowingly.

'I still can't believe you're going back to wiping out rats and mice again, luvvy. Still, I suppose you won't be so hands-on this time.'

'It's what I do. Any which way, I've got so much going on, this will occupy about two days a week. Then I've got all my other stuff to sort out.'

'Oh, I totally forgot. Talking about stuff you have to sort out, Central News, BBC telly, Radio Derby and Ram FM were on the phone. They all want to do an interview with you about taking over Derby County and becoming chairman. I told them to all pop round at half past one. That's OK, isn't it?'

'Aye, it is. I can't wait for Saturday. Home to cowing Plymouth Argyle in the Cup at Pride Park. My first match as chairman and major shareholder.'

'You'll be picking the team next, luvvy.'

'No, I'll leave that to our new manager, Sven. He's had enough experience. Any which way, we're paying him enough cowing dough.'

Barbara relished her new role as wife and PA.

'Now, I'm going to perc some coffee, then I've got to make some final checks about the catering and guest list tonight. We've had very few cancellations. Let's see... We've got the Mayor of Derby, Sven, four local MPs and assorted local dignitaries. Smudger and Oops are coming up from London. Biffo, of course, won't be there. Streaky is popping along, thankfully without the snobby, stuck-up Arabella. I've got the champagne ready for opening at six and some fantastic food, including those samosas you love. So we're all systems go.'

The banner was spread across the entire front of the pub. 'Official opening of the newly refurbished Ferret and Bicycle. New owner

165

and landlord, the legendary Lenny Peabody of the Dogs and Peabody's Pest Control'.

The landlord was in top form, his drinking arm fully recovered. Poddy shunned the champers and canapés and joined Big Eric and Little Jimmy over three pint-pots in a corner of the re-styled mock Tudor bar. The terminator, inseminator and exterminator were back in session amid the horse brasses, pewter mugs and hunting prints of a genuine country pub. Heaven.

'As a bailiff, Big Eric, you could get some work at Pride Park by expelling a few useless items, namely half the cowing squad.'

'Only half the squad? More like three-quarters. That overweight Russian striker, Vladimir whatsisfaceov, gets round more bars in a week than we used to on holiday in Skegness. He empties so many bottles that the council are putting a recycling plant outside his house. The story is that he's out of the next match 'cos he's pissed a fatness test.'

Little Jimmy piped in.

'Then there's that useless Colombian, Lopez. They reckon he's already had a benefit from three clubs: the Pink Coconut, Roosters and Harleys in Derby city centre. If he spent a little more time on the training ground and less in night clubs, he might be some sodding use.'

Big Eric drained the rest of his pint.

'D'you realise, Poddy, that last week we put out a side with everyone speaking a different bastard language? The problem was hardly anyone could speak a word of English. Even the skipper, Fortunatio, only manages to say hello, goodbye, pass and shoot. We had one Columbian, one Brazilian, one Italian, a Romanian, one Czech guy, one Russian, a Korean, a Serbian, one Hungarian, a Tunisian and the Greek boy.'

Poddy looked puzzled. 'My God, things have changed since I've been away. How do they communicate?'

Big Eric looked thoughtful. 'Well, I think it's by pointing and sign language when they're in the clubs and bars. On the field they don't fucking bother.'

Little Jimmy nodded in agreement.

'There're so many foreign TV and radio people hanging around, it looks like a UN meeting on every match day. I keep expecting Kofi Annan to turn up. Can you believe three crews came from Korea last week to cover Sun Ee Jim's debut? At least he looks a prospect.'

Poddy was bemused. These were his players with his club, but he hadn't heard of half of them.

'Well, I've found out that some of them know a few rudimentary words of English. They don't realise I'm in charge yet. I asked that skinny Italian, Olivetti, for a couple of words and he said "fuck off". He thought it was very funny. Any which way, he won't be laughing too much when he needs his contract renegotiating next month; the skiving bastard will be on his bike back to Brindisi.

'Anyway, lads: there's this Frenchman, Italian and Geordie discussing love-making. The Frenchman says, "After making love to my wife I cover her body with soft cream and lick it off slowly and she goes absolutely crazy." The Italian says, "After making love to my wife I cover her body with soft feathers and blow them off slowly. She goes absolutely mad." Then the Geordie says, "After I make love to my wife, I wipe my dick on the curtains and she goes absolutely potty".'

The exterminator, terminator and inseminator guffawed loudly. Poddy clicked his fingers and three more pints were delivered to the landlord's table.

It was a sharp and bright morning. A skinny, bony figure clad in an army camouflage anorak was returning to an isolated whitewashed farmhouse embedded high in the Derbyshire hills. The man was followed by two sedate Labradors. The surrounding fells produced a sharp, dark edge against the pale blue sky.

Charlie 'Biffo' Bear took his boots off in the porch of the house and cleaned the dogs' feet with a wet towel. He walked through the hallway to a large pine kitchen.

'Fookin' great morning, Sylvie. Hardly saw a bloody soul. There were two ramblers coming down the path by the river, but I walked over the bridge to avoid the bastards. Otherwise it was just me, Lambert, Perkin, the birds, bees and beasts.'

'How far did you walk, luvvy?'

'Aye, well, we must have done about five miles at the very

least, no bother at all and not had to speak to anyone. Long may that continue. Anyway, Lambert's puffing a bit.'

'That's fantastic. Dr Robert will be ever so pleased. Your latest results after last week's check were excellent. They don't want to see you again for six months.'

'Aye, I've never felt better, and thank god we don't have to go to that fookin' congested rabbit warren of a hospital for a while.'

'Well, let's keep it up. Here's your breakfast. A bowl of muesli, skimmed milk and mixed fruit.'

Biffo frowned.

'Could still do with a big bacon buttie rather than this rabbit food.'

'Well, you're allowed one monster buttie on Sunday with all the fat trimmed off. Otherwise fry-ups are strictly out of order, Charles.'

Biffo grunted. 'Anything in the post?'

'Nothing much. Just confirmation that we've received another five million in royalties that have been paid into the bank. Oh, and Lambert and Perkin need to go to the vet in Ashbourne on Wednesday for their regular jabs and check-ups.'

'Well, you can do that, Sylvie. I can't stand that supercilious arse of a vet and his stupid receptionist who sounds like a fookin' foghorn. Her voice could fracture your skull. And all the bastards there want my autograph.'

'Now, now, calm down. At least the vet, Mr Blatherwick, has a good reputation. He's marvellous with animals.'

'Aye, that he might be, but he's a condescending bastard to people. Arrogant git, I don't like him.'

'Well, I need to load up at the supermarket on Wednesday, so I'll take the Land Rover. By the way, remember the Shaws from the Crescent? They're popping in to see us for morning coffee tomorrow.'

'Well, remind me to miss them. Not silly-Billy and tawdry-Audrey Shaw. I'll be out with Lambert and Perkin. We'll be back when they clear off. Anyway, we've got that fireplace company arriving at eleven thirty to fix the two big log fires.'

Biffo got up from the table and started to ferret about in the kitchen.

'Sylvie, have you seen my book on Ho Chi Minh?'

'Luvvy, it's where you left it in the downstairs loo. Now, once we've had breakfast, we can relax in front of the fire and read the papers. I'll make some fresh tea – I think both Lambert and Perkin are spark out. You really must have taken them for a long hike.'

'Aye, like me they're not getting any younger. In fact, according to dog ages, we're all about the same vintage. As there're seven dog years to a human year, me, Lambert and Perkin are all seventy.'

'Well, at least you're seventy and fabulously rich, Charlie Bear, and you shouldn't have a worry in the world.'

'Aye, well, I've worried all my fookin' life, so I'm not going to stop now.'

It was an hour after dawn on a warm June morning. The mist still clung to a cleft on the Shropshire Canal. A tall wiry figure jogged along the towpath alongside an exquisitely painted green and yellow narrowboat. The runner was clad in a grey woolly hat, with his straggly salt-and-pepper hair hanging over his ears and down to the collar of his royal blue sweatshirt. He wore grey knee-length shorts and heavily padded blue and white trainers.

As he bobbed along he chatted to a tall, slim, raven-haired woman steering the boat.

'Look, babe, I'll run for two miles, then we'll swap over, you run and I'll man the boat. "You know you're floating in a most peculiar way and the sun looks very different today".'

'So I can man, or rather woman, the boat for a bit longer. Then when I've had my jog I've got a special surprise, big boy. We're having some pancakes with strawberries and organic Columbian coffee with fresh cream.'

James 'Smudger' Smith and Olivia Olga Ponsonby-Smart had virtually been an item since the Dogs' tour of America. Since returning to Britain, they had bought a splendid apartment in Mayfair, a remote farmhouse with a recording studio and a custom-built narrowboat. They had decided to live on the boat during June, July and August and divide the rest of their time between the London base and the farmhouse.

Smudger had signed up various bands and assorted artists to

produce, while Oops had built up a portfolio of PR contacts.

As he paced along the canal, Smudger swung his arms in a circular motion.

'"Keep on running". "It's a beautiful daayyy!"'

Oops popped her head up from the tiller.

'You must have run well over two miles by now. I think there's a lock another half a mile ahead or so.'

'This is just great, babe. I remember when I was in the Hollywood Hills recording and jamming with Frank Zappa, Ginger Baker and Gerry Garcia. While those cats were chilling out after recording, I used to go for a long run with two of the recording engineers. We used to tie on big flowery bandanas and wear those gaudy tracksuits with all the colours of the rainbow. It was like a freaks' athletics club. I don't know if I ever told you, but at that time I was also doing sessions with Crosby, Stills, Nash, Young and Smith.'

Oops grinned and flicked back her long, lush dark hair. She delighted in hearing Smudger's tales, even for the umpteenth time.

'You know, this air is just like a kind of nectar gas, babe. There's no drug can give you this kinda trip. I remember telling young Kurty, Kurt Cobain, that he ought to move away, miles from anyone near Seattle and take it easy and not get so strung out, man.'

Oops craned her neck and peered down the canal.

'We're close to Wales.'

'Don't fret, babe; this water's far too shallow for whales.'

Smudger laughed out loud at his own joke as he continued jogging along the flinty towpath.

'You're the chick who makes me tick, babe, you're right, we're less than a mile from Wales; that's where my old mate Jonesey comes from. I tell you, we're going to moor alongside a fantastic pub tonight and have a few glasses of red and some top-class tucker, babe.'

'Your mate Jonesey from Wales; that wouldn't be Tom, by any chance?'

'That's my man, Oops.'

In the front room of a large modern version of a Victorian mansion backing on to Darley Vale golf club, two men in brown coats were delivering some antique furniture. Arabella Bacon was barking out instructions.

'If you could be very careful with that, the chaise longue goes into the bay window of the drawing room. Yes, that's it, just a tad to the left. Now, if you can collect the Welsh dresser that fits against the wall in the right hand corner of the kitchen. That's the corner with the Aga facing you.'

Streaky hovered in the back room as Arabella hectored the delivery men. It took a ridiculously long time to get the pieces in place. After the men left, Arabella's voice echoed around the house.

'Brian, Brian! Coffee is served in the drawing room.'

Streaky strode in carrying a golf putter in his hand and staring absentmindedly at it.

'I don't know if this will be the answer, but I'll try it out.'

Arry poured coffee from an elaborate cafetière and they began a conversation in parallel: one line after another, with neither person listening to the other. This was togetherness in the Bacon household.

'Well, we've got this whole sorry, sordid Dogs' saga to thank for all this. But thank god it's all over and life is back to normal. It's been like a reality TV show or some sort of survival test.'

'I suppose I could try that new driver that Wally showed me in the pro shop. That could gain me a few yards off the tee.'

Arry continued her own conversation, seemingly oblivious to her husband.

'By the way, don't be too late back from the clubhouse tonight. Dot and Maurice are popping round for a wine and bridge soirée.'

'You know, with a bit more work on my putting... I think inconsistency is the problem. I could cure that and get my handicap back into single figures.'

'By the way, did I tell you that Squiffy and Suki are getting back together?'

'One difficulty is that new greenkeeper has left things a bit lush. I suppose with all the rain we've had, that's not surprising, but I like slick greens. Well, I mean not as slick as Augusta, Georgia.'

'Nigel's going into hospital next week to have his hip done. We'll have to pop in and see him and take some fruit and flowers.'

'I spoke to Johnny Freemantle; he's had this set of custom-built clubs made, every one designed to his specifications. That's now an option I can afford.'

'Oh, that new vicar at St Botolph's has been causing a stir. Do you know he's been having a bit of hanky panky with that brassy woman who runs the crematorium? She's been divorced twice, you know. Dot says she's had a boob job and a face-lift. Bloody cheap job, too; can't tell if she's glaring or smiling.'

'Wally says if I can keep up my form from the tee and brush up my putting, then who knows, I could be playing off seven or eight. Anyway, I can't wait to try out this putter. It's an old one. Quite a long way back, Monty used to have one just like it in his bag.'

Something in Arabella's consciousness latched onto this last sentence.

'I didn't know that Field Marshall Montgomery was a great golfer.'

'Eh?' Now it was Streaky's turn to acknowledge that his wife was in the room.

'Montgomery? Oh, no, no, Arry. Not that Monty. I mean Colin Montgomerie, the famous Scottish golfer.'

'Oh, golf. For a minute I thought you were talking about something of importance. As you know, anything about golf is lost on me. I used to like that Jack Nicklaus and the only other golfer I've heard of is Tiger Woods. Anyway, good news for you. Mr Jepson has put that gate in at the back of the garden. So you can walk straight onto the course.'

'Yes, marvellous. It's about three hundred and fifty yards to the clubhouse. We've got this committee meeting this evening.'

They were, for once, on the same conversational path.

'Don't forget Dot and Maurice, and you're doing that lunch-time Mozart recital for my Conservative ladies' luncheon club. It's a sell-out at seventy-five pounds a ticket. We should raise £20,000 for the children's hospital.'

Streaky smiled weakly.

'Well, I've got a full diary. My classical concert tour is sold out. I'll barely get two rounds of golf in this week.'

★

Twelve months later

While it was blue skies all the way for the Dogs, storm clouds were gathering over the HQ of Jet Records in New York. Managing Director Brett Radische thumped the table triumphantly. He had a vindictive grin on his face.

'We've got the goddamn bastards. So those Limey sons of bitches thought they could haul their asses back to England for tea and scones and worm their way out of a goddamn contract. May, you're so goddamn good. Bring us up to date.'

May Moon, the twenty-five-year-old daughter of Vietnamese immigrants, coolly opened a leather-bound file on the desk. She'd learned long ago that Westerners like Radische only respected people who could give them what they craved – and what they craved was money and power over other people. She made sure she gave them both.

'Well, first we wrote letters to all four members of the band and their manager, Buddy Peabody, pointing out they were still under contract to complete a new album, live DVD and European Tour. They wrote back via their lawyers to say they hadn't signed a contract and the Dogs were now disbanded.'

Radische thumped the table again with glee.

'Yeah, well, that's what the goddamn old boy chappies thought, but we've got the crooked-teeth bastards over a barrel, and I believe, May, that it's an absolutely watertight barrel. Am I right?'

'No doubt about that, Mr Radische. First, I managed to dig up this.' She held up a piece of paper. 'It's a letter of intent from Buddy Peabody saying that they totally agree to everything in the new contract. So that proves the contracts were drawn up, and, due to an oversight, or rather inefficiency, they were not signed. We've actually got a TV interview with James Smith, the hairy hippy guy, saying they're delighted with the new deal and can't wait to work on the new album, DVD and European tour.'

Brett Radische's thin, malevolent smile was getting broader.

'Any objections to this, Bentley?'

Bentley Gardner shook his head. 'Well, no, except it's a year or so on, and the band are now aged between sixty-four and seventy-one. Can they still do it? They've been in retirement for over a year.'

May Moon pulled several pieces of paper from her file.

'Age isn't a legal issue here. We've got other pieces of correspondence agreeing to the contract and transcripts from a series of radio interviews where members of the band say they're delighted with the new terms.'

Radische shuddered the table with several thumps of a right fist encrusted with gold rings.

'You bet your ass they were delighted with the new terms! Not as delighted as I am right now. They'll be out of retirement very soon. These goddamn Limey seniors owe us big time. We're going to work the bastards to death.'

Treat Me like a Dog

Like a good old dog I'm trusty and true
Baby I'm just far too good for you
You give a whistle and I come running
I'm just faithful and you're so cunning
Cos you treat me like a dog
Treat me like a dog
You've got me yelping and yapping, snarling and a snapping
Cos you treat me like a dog
I go for walkies when you tell porkies
Cos when the fur flies you tell lies
Your bite's much worse than your bark
You've got me groping in the dark
Cos you treat me like a dog
Treat me like a dog
You've got me yelping and yapping, snarling and a snapping
Cos you treat me like a dog
I'm just a poodle, you're like a hound
I'm on the leash when you're around
C'mon baby just stop that nagging
All you need is to get my tail wagging
Cos you treat me like a dog
Treat me like a dog
You've got me yelping and yapping, snarling and a snapping
Cos you treat me like a dog

Printed in the United Kingdom
by Lightning Source UK Ltd.
118548UK00001B/22-66